THORNS OF PIETY

Thorns Of Piety

E.G. BOYLAN

ISBN-13: 9781733342926
Cover design by: Elisabeth Boylan.
Library of Congress Control Number: TXu 2-445-392

First Printing August 31, 2024

"I am completely trapped," Susanna groaned. "If I yield, it will be my death; if I refuse, I cannot escape your power. Yet it is better for me not to do it and to fall into your power than to sin before the Lord."

THE BOOK OF DANIEL - CHAPTER 13: 22-23

$\sim 1 \sim$

THE CHALICE

It's 1983 on a Sunday morning in an idyllic gated community, with a curving network of streets and bike paths named after the most scenic areas of France. A French-speaking town with just a sprinkle of anglophone families who had not followed the exodus. These holdouts, endearingly referred to *par les Québécois* as *des bloques, des maudites anglais, ou les têtes carrées.*

The Bailey Family was of Irish descent through the father, Frank Bailey, and had a maternal mix of Irish and French through Liliane (née Taillefer), who was raised by the Grey Nuns of Montréal.

Their home was a four-bedroom, single-story California-style bungalow with an asymmetric angled roof and floor-to-ceiling windows in the living room that dominated the front facade. A mix of maple trees and evergreens framed the house and the carport covered a dog house for the family dog, an Irish Setter named Cana.

The front lawn serving as a testament to Frank Bailey's environmental stance against pesticides, was covered with dandelions. And a large family station wagon with wood panels was parked in the asphalt driveway.

A window is opened from the Master Bedroom, and a song, "De Colores" by Nana Mouskouri, becomes audible. Inside, Liliane is preparing for Sunday morning service at St. Patrick's Basilica. She sings along to 'Dec Colores'. An anthem for the Cursillo movement, a hippyish cult-like subset of 'Catholicism'. Where initiates adopt a boundless idealism that *We are all brothers and sisters in Christ.*

In the living room, the children, Shannon the eldest at fifteen years old, Tommy, thirteen years old, and the youngest, Grace Liliane Bailey at seven years old, are hypnotically being transported to the Next Frontier, watching an episode of Star Trek. Their father wearing a brown suit, walks into the living room, stands by the television to put an end to their journey, "Turn the TV off. We are leaving for Church in 10 minutes."

Frank, an electrical engineer by profession, carries a nuclear load of regret for his past work with Boeing Missile Defence. He was introduced to his wife, Liliane by a matchmaker Priest privileged to each of their private confessions. In addition to making an attractive couple, the Priest believed the magnitude of burden they carried for their errors was a mutual opportunity for salvation through the sacrament of Marriage.

In front of a vanity mirror above a wide dresser in the Master Bedroom, Liliane applies her mascara. Compared to the wedding photo that dutifully remains on her dresser of the couple eating wedding cake, Liliane in middle age is now an over-endowed, voluptuous woman.

She wears a beige slip, beige pantyhose, and smart beige Naturalizer heels. Wondering to herself if she could just lose this weight, confused at the cause for the added mass. A bad memory revisits her mind of a male Parishioner, "Liliane, if you could lose all that weight, you would look like a movie star! You'd be stunning!" She removes her plastic curlers. Her hair is big curls on a short strawberry blond bob. She applies her lipstick and, in a nanosecond split of character, winks at herself in the mirror and smiles glamorously at the thought of what could have been.

Reaching for her cross necklace just as Grace, her youngest daughter, comes into her room wearing a pink frilly dress with white patent leather shoes that *click click click* as she walks.

As Liliane carefully attaches her necklace chain behind her neck, Grace points to the elaborate box on the bed, "What's that?"

Liliane moves to sit on the bed and open the box for Grace, "It's something splendid for Jesus," she says in a delighted voice, whispering with excitement, "It cost a fortune!" Liliane opens the engraved wood box from the top; inside is a purple velvet encasing for a gold Chalice with a jewel at its stem. Grace reaches for the box, and her mother slaps her hand. "Don't touch! It's for Mass today; you'll get fingerprints on it."

In a kind of trance, Liliane says, "Father Dale is going to bless it. And every time it's used, it will be a prayer. Something I just had to get for the Church." Every time her mother mentions that name, Grace experiences an uneasy confusion. An unpleasant feeling that overwhelms her comprehension. "But why?" Grace asks.

Liliane takes the Chalice out to hold it for Grace to see it up close in its splendour. The light from the window shines off the cup and penetrates the jewel at the stem. "You see this? It's beautiful, right? *Grace, Mummy is the diamond.* Each time there's a Mass, I'll be lifted up by Dale, by Father Dale. So it's very special and means so much more than any of the other Chalices."

Unconvinced, Grace asks, "Mum, how much did it cost?"

Liliane, irritated by Grace's lack of enthusiasm, shoos her away, "Get out! Get out! Go wash your hands; they're filthy. Then get into the car."

Frank is patiently waiting in the station wagon, tapping the steering wheel while contemplating the passage of time. He watches Grace come out and say goodbye to the family dog, kissing her head and petting her red coat. "Bye Cana! I'm going to miss you. We'll come back and take you for a walk."

Grace holds a treat up as Tommy comes out. Forever competing, Tommy beckons the excitable setter, jumping with excitement and patting his thighs to sway Cana away from his little sister. "Come Cana, come here! Come! Come!"

Cana runs to Tommy. Strategically inaudible to his father, Tommy taunts his little sister, "See how she loves me, Grace? Proof, she loves me more than you. More than even that treat in your hand. You know why? Because you're nothing inside and I am everything! She only pays attention to you if I am not around."

As she steps out of the house, Shannon overhears the exchange. Grace is disheartened. Intervening, "Tommy, what are you saying? You realize you're six years older than her and you have to compete with her over the affection of Cana. What's wrong with you?" Cana runs to Shannon to be pet.

"Yah! What's wrong with you Tommy?" Grace exclaims loud enough for Frank to hear.

Tommy chases Grace to the car and pinches her until she cries out with a screech beside Frank's open window. Startling her father, "GRACE! Do you have to screech like that? The neighbours!"

Grace pleads his sympathy, "Dad, he pinched me!" Tommy, his hands open and incredulous, "I barely touched her! The Baby!"

They all slide into the station wagon's vinyl backseat, awaiting their Mother. Liliane opens the front door, holding up a picnic basket to summon her husband. Frank exits the car, slowly walking to fetch the 'lunch' Liliane has prepared. The basket weighs heavily on his psyche, like an anchor descending him into the abyss as he carries it to his car. Frank ruefully looks at the basket before shutting the trunk.

Returning to the driver's seat, his kids are in the back. Tommy is aggressively shoving Grace, who is seated in the middle. "Move over stupid! I don't want your dress frills touching my leg." Grace pulls her dress under her leg and squeezes as close to her older sister to avoid Tommy's wrath.

Liliane finally approaches, walking slowly along the garden path in her heels, a cream blouse with a pussy bow and long skirt. She holds the Chalice box against her chest as her purse hangs from her right elbow. As she struggles to open the passenger car door, she becomes irritated with Frank for his delayed assistance. Unlocking his seat belt, Frank leans over to open and awkwardly shove the passenger door open from inside.

Liliane slips in and shuts the door. She looks over to Frank with disdain, letting out a sigh of frustration to announce, "There's a lasagna for you in the fridge for after mass." A loaded subtext: *I made lunch for you too, Frank.*

Frank gives a single silent nod. He turns the key in the ignition, letting the engine roar for him as he puts his arm over Liliane's passenger seat to reverse out of the driveway.

It's a slow drive to Church with the speed limit of 30 km/ hour in their hometown. Stops at every intersection, with a red sign that exclaims 'ARRET!'.

Tommy breaks the silence, "I'm serving notice. Today's the last time I'll be an altar server."

Liliane, still infused with a self-generated mix of cortisol, adrenaline, and contempt for having to open her passenger door, begins to criticize Frank and blame him for Tommy's defiance and behavior. She bickers with him the whole drive about what is wrong with their son and how he isn't disciplining him properly. Frank attempts to evade the discussion, seeking not to further fuel Liliane's addiction to conflict with any resistance. This infuriates her more, as she thinks to herself: *There he goes, St. Francis playing the martyr, turning the other cheek. More points for you at the Gates of St. Peter.*

The family station wagon arrives at the church parking lot along with the arrival of other Parishioners. Liliane steps out at the same time as Shannon and Tommy. Meanwhile, Frank recuperates for a moment with Grace.

Liliane says, "Tommy, go prepare." As he runs up the steps to the front entrance she calls out a stern warning, "Tommy? Tommy?" He turns, and she warns, " Don't embarrass me."

Inside the car, Grace leans over from the back of the driver's seat to wrap her arms around her father. Sunday morning drives to this Church have become tense between her parents. "Dad, I like the French church better. I find him creepy, and he smells." Frank chuckles and shakes his head before kissing her little hand. Confessing to her, "Me too."

Perhaps the Irish Melancholy is to blame for Frank's inclination to his dutiful suffering at St. Patrick's. His thoughts inevitably wander during mass, so what would be the difference if the Mass were all in French? The French Church, Notre Dame, is a closer drive. Its Parishioners don't trigger the same politics or competitive display of spiritual performance or even a hierarchy of donation status. Father L'Heureux, a jovial and welcoming priest, evokes a young french version of Santa Claus, with his glasses, long brown beard and big hair. Rather than an ostentatious purple and gold robe, he sets a humble tone by wearing sandals under a simple white robe. Preaching as an equal to his congregation.

But *Notre Dame* was a French Church, and Frank Bailey was a *tête carrée*.

Shannon enters church just ahead of her mother and brother, who have walked down a separate hallway to the Sacristy. The interior of St. Patrick's is an elaborate combination of vaulted ceilings, mahogany pews, and wood confessional booths on opposite sides. A long marble nave aisle leads to the marble altar with green and gold accents surrounding the large stained glass lancet windows that feature art depicting the Patron Saints, St. Patrick and St. Brigid of Kildare, and of course all fourteen Stations of the Cross.

As Shannon walks up the left side aisle, a parishioner and frenemy of her mother Liliane, Vicki Bergeron, exits the confessional booth on the far opposite. Vicki walks to the candle vigil at the opposite corner of the Altar. After depositing a coin, she makes a sign of the cross before lighting a candle and kneeling to pray. Shannon watches to then see Father Dale exit from the confessional, rushing to the Sacristy as he nods and winks his approval to Mrs. Bergeron.

Before choosing a pew, Shannon walks up the opposite side aisle to the Red candle vigil. She wonders what prayer Mrs. Bergeron made and what each candle might represent and by which parishioner.

She takes a seat in the front pew, left of the Altar. Looking up at the Statue of Mary, her little sister playfully slides into the pew beside her. With an appalled expression, Grace whispers referring to Mary, "She was only twelve!"

Shannon replies matter-of-factly, "Grace, back then they were ALL only twelve. Sometimes younger." Grace's mouth drops open at the thought, holding her tummy.

Mrs. Bergeron walks over to greet Shannon and Grace. In a syrupy sweet voice through a stiff smile, she says, "Hello Shannon! Grace, don't you look pretty in your pink dress? Shannon, what I would give to have your hair!"

Her evaluating gaze shifts between the two sisters, "Are your mother and father here?"

"Yes, they're coming," Shannon replies, anticipating the next question.

"Wonderful!" She feigns delight with exaggerated enthusiasm. Now snooping, "Shannon, I hear you're applying for scholarships? What schools?"

"Mostly out West. But a couple in the US," Shannon is reticent to provide her mom's arch-nemesis any information that will somehow circle back by causing her mom added frustration. Vicki, astonished, "That's far, Shannon! You won't miss home?" Shannon shrugs indifferently. Vicki continues, "My advice is don't get your heart set on just one school. Have a backup plan because you never know."

"Thank you, Mrs. Bergeron. That's good advice," Shannon responds politely.

The nuance of female-on-female aggression in the form of questions or underhanded commentary is a delicate terrain. The patterns of which Shannon has begun to identify and navigate. A subtle warfare waged with sentences that may include or begin with: *Are you sure?... I was under the impression.... Is that so?... that's concerning...Well, I heard...*

As Vicki Bergeron trots off with a forced smile and wave, defiance stirs inside Shannon. The pitch of her voice saying *'That's far'* echoes in her ears. In retaliation, she imagines herself blowing out Mrs. Bergeron's vigil candle and then ALL the candles.

Laughing irreverent at all the parishioners crying for their unanswered prayers. Her father scolding her and Father Dale shaking his head with disapproval. Shannon catches herself in a giggle that grows into an uncontrollable laugh that she has to cover with her hand.

Her friend, Nat, arrives with her family and is waving curiously to her from across the aisle.

~ 2 ~

THE BLESSING

In the Sacristy, just as Father Dale enters from hearing confessions, Liliane is waiting to hand him her Chalice. Not yet in his purple and gold cassock and his stole, he is wearing his regular black shirt and pants with his white collar. Father Dale places the Chalice on the counter, opens the box, and performs a sign of the cross, issuing a blessing upon it.

Looking at Liliane, smiling and pointing to the diamond in the Chalice's stem, "This is you. This jewel represents how you are truly a diamond in the rough. And I will raise you up!"

Liliane, flustered with emotion, lets out a sigh of relief. She looks at him in adoring limerence. Unable to fathom how her vulnerability is at the root of this idealization, she believes this magical ritual will lead to a personal salvation, where she can be raised above all her sorrow.

Tommy, just in time, walks in from around the corner

wearing his altar server robe and a sardonic smirk. Accustomed to his mother's infatuation, he's swinging his robe's rope. Interrupting, "Father Dale, I am giving notice. Today is my last day as an altar server. I need Sundays to focus my energy and time as an *artist*."

Father Dale replies in his patronizing and paternalistic tone, "Yes, Tommy my son. The time has come, young man. As I have experience with the arts, your mother has asked me to come over to see your paintings so that I can guide you in your path. Any talent is a God-given gift that must be cultivated so that it truly may serve God's Will. Like Michelangelo. I am delighted that I will have a hand in molding your craft."

Tommy stands with silent consternation.

Liliane, putting her hand on Tommy's shoulder, "Tommy, isn't that wonderful? Father Dale will be over for dinner and you can show him what you're working on. Our Michelangelo!"

Waving her hands good-bye, "I'll leave you both and see you after mass." Liliane walks back to the Church to find Shannon, Grace, and Frank in a pew that is off-centre. She insists that they switch over with the family at the centre pew. Front row seats, so to speak.

Liliane approaches the woman, appealing to her good nature, "Hi Diane, Could we switch seats? Mass includes a blessing for our family. I would like to be able to see better. It's Tommy's last time as an altar server..., he's going to focus on *his art*."

Diane accommodatingly, "Not at all, Liliane. Of course." The woman and her two daughters trade places with Frank, Shannon, and Grace who cross the aisle to slip in beside Liliane who has taken her seat. Liliane is smiling, pleased with herself for taking charge.

The organ music begins with an uninspiring hymn. Disappointed, Grace wonders why they don't choose the best hymns instead of the boring ones that no one wants to sing.

At the front of the procession, Tommy is holding the processional crucifix, a cross that is atop a long pole. The altar boy behind him is dutifully holding up the Bible above his head. Two Eucharistic ministers in white robes follow, and at the end of the procession is Father Dale. Walking slowly, he blesses members of his congregation as he walks up the nave to the Altar.

Shannon turns to casually look at Nat's older brother, Sebastian. He's home from school. She admires how his tousled brown locks kissed just below his brow. And the way his scholarly tweed blazer draped perfectly across his swim-meet shoulders. She recalls swim team practice, and staring at how the beads of water would roll over his tanned skin.

Grace can barely handle the monotony. She looks around at other parishioners. She wonders what they think of her mother's Chalice. She follows, just as everyone sits, stands, or kneels. Waiting for the three events. First, when everyone has to shake hands with their neighbour and wish them peace.   To Grace, this was by far the worst part ever of every mass. Dreading how sweaty her palms will be when she has to shake hands and wish her neighbour, 'Peace be with you'. If only she could have dry hands? She spends the time leading up to this ritual, waving her hands at her sides and blowing on them, cringing.

The second event is when the money is collected as an offering to be blessed by Father Dale. That's when Frank allows Grace to put the envelope of money, called a tithe, into the basket.

Last, but not least, The Holy Eucharist. Having made her First Communion, Grace was now permitted to partake in the Mass snack, otherwise known as "The Body Of Christ." The Eucharist wafer tasted no different from the packaged wafers she bought from the *dépanneur*. She and her friends would joke while eating their bag of candies 'the body Christ', repeatedly imitating the priest, lifting it up, laughing, and eating the wafer.

Grace pondered, how might the Eucharist taste today? Maybe there would be a godly magic from today's blessing that was perceptible because it was done in her family's Chalice?

~ 3 ~

HOLY 'UNHOLY' COMMUNION

Father Dale is at the Altar blessing the Eucharist. He raises up the Chalice high above his head to capture the light. Just then, as if by magic, a hidden bell is rung from the side by the diligent Altar Server next to Tommy.

Father Dale, with dramatic authority, proclaims, "Take this, all of you, and drink from it. This is the cup of My Blood, the Blood of the new and everlasting covenant!" Revealing the sacred vessel to his attentive Parishioners, he then drinks from the Chalice, making eye contact with Liliane, smiling at her reassuringly as though to say, 'It is done. I have drunk from your Chalice.'

Frank slowly turns his gaze to study Liliane's reaction. Keenly aware of his observation, she puts her head down in prayer, says "Amen." Making the sign of the cross, before looking forward again.

As the organ plays a hymn, the congregation lines up to kneel at the Communion rail. A holy fence separating the Altar from the Nave, with a cushioned velvet bench to kneel upon. While waiting for the Eucharist, some parishioners hold out their hand, others prepare to hold out their tongue.

Tommy's task as the altar server is to hold a golden plate under their chin to catch the Eucharist wafer should it accidentally slip off their tongue. As he does this, Tommy witnesses a dimension of prolonged eye contact between Mrs. Bergeron and Father Dale, "The Body of Christ, Vicki."

At thirteen, he doesn't quite know what to make of whose name Father Dale decides to say as he places the wafer upon their tongue. All he knows is, it's something hilarious to imitate. As much as it is the women who dote on him seeking his approval. Tragically, one of these being his mother, Liliane.

Moving along to give out communion, Father Dale and Tommy approach his family. Frank, Shannon, and Grace are holding out their hands. While Liliane, is opting to receive the Eucharist on her tongue with that worshipful desperate look on her face. "The Body of Christ, Liliane" Father Dale says with an extra special intonation.

Tommy's head goes faint with a simultaneous plummet in his gut. Embarrassment clouding his focus, he thinks, *I can't wait for this to be over.* After the rite of communion, Tommy and the other altar boy are charged with 'clean up' duties, one of these returning the Chalice to the Sacristy.

While the whole of the Parish is still in prayer, a loud noise echoes from the altar. Tommy has dropped the Chalice on the Marble floor; it clangs and rolls and bounces. His mother cringes and puts her head in her hands in horrified disbelief. Tommy stumbles forward to pick the Chalice up, 'accidentally' kicks it, it clangs and rolls, he chases it. 'Accidentally' kicks it again. Tommy looks over to his mother who is a mix of injured, desperate fury and embarrassment. Father Dale is equally unimpressed and sternly looks on, shaking his head at Tommy.

Shannon, sitting beside her father and little sister, is holding back her laughter, watching her brother, Tommy, holding back his laugh, trying to appear earnest and remorseful as he picks up the Chalice. Holds it up to inspect if he has made a dent in it. Pursing his lips together like his father. The crystal is chipped, and there are sacrilegious dents in the gold cup.

Father Dale sternly looks on, shaking his head while looking to Tommy's father, Frank. Tommy brings the Chalice to the Sacristy and returns to his seat on the altar, ignoring Father Dale's disapproving glare. Nay, reveling in his disapproval, as his lips twitch in his attempt to conceal amusement.

Father Dale rises, opening his arms to his Parishioners, and makes the sign of the cross in a wide-reaching blessing, "May almighty God bless you, the Father, and the Son, and the Holy Spirit!"

With the clang of the Chalice still echoing, the congregation responds with a solemn, "Amen!"

"The Mass is ended, go in peace, to love and serve the Lord! Thanks be to God. Amen!"

Father Dale makes a final announcement, that he will meet with his Parishioners at the front entrance. But first and foremost, there is his altar boy, whom he must discipline.

Performing an encore, Tommy retrieves the processional crucifix to lead his final Processional exit. As he marches, Tommy meets his gaze with his sister and then his friends in the pews, sharing a silent and rebellious celebration. Once in the Sacristy, Father Dale scolds Tommy about the sanctity that his mother's Chalice represents.

They are standing in front of a large glass door cabinet, full of gold and platinum Chalices, with labels of each family name for the respective donation. A clear display of how the Church was not in need of yet another gold Chalice.

Liliane has rushed back to the Sacristy. She is crying, looking over the Chalice being dusted and polished by the silent Monk. There are multiple dents in it, and the Crystal is cracked. "Oh no," she laments. She pleads with the Monk who is dusting and polishing her Chalice, pressuring him to break his vow of silence. Desperate, "Can it be fixed? Is it possible to repair it?" Liliane's intense attachment and infatuation with Father Dale's promise of the magic within her Chalice is on full display to the silent Monk. Her disappointment enrages her toward her son, Tommy.

The Monk remains silent yet sympathetic to Liliane. For he himself has witnessed the impropriety of Father Dale using donated Chalices to convey special messages of favouritism to his female parishioners.

Liliane, sniffling to Father Dale, "He's so awful and disobedient. His father just stands by while he misbehaves and abuses his little sister. He thinks it's funny. If only you were his Father?"

Father Dale, embracing Liliane's hand within his, "Liliane, I am Tommy's *spiritual* father, and I will continue to guide him where Frank fails."

Outside the Church, Grace asks Shannon if she found the Eucharist tasted different for being blessed in Mum's Cup. Shannon pleads with her father, "Why did you let her spend $1000 on that cup?"

Frank, walks shaking his head in dismay. Recovering from Tommy's accidental performance that exposed the impractical and ungodly silliness of such an expense.

Shouting from two cars over, Bob Bergeron hollers out, "Frank, it isn't the first time he's misbehaved in Church. Maybe you ought to let him convert?"

Tommy approaches the family vehicle, complacently descending the front steps, "It was an accident!" To his sister, "You never dropped anything?"

Shannon replies, "And then kicked it? No." Turning to her father, "You guys criticize me for buying a Ralph Lauren blouse with my own babysitting money, and then you buy a cup made of gold for Father Dale? When he has a cabinet full of them donated by other hopeless wives! It'll just be left there for the monk to dust every week. He'll just use it to string mom along!"

Frank, unable to disagree, "Shannon, spend your money as you wish. As long as you're not breaking a commandment to earn it. You are to honor your mother and father. Do not question or undermine our decisions. Your saucy tone and choice of words are disrespectful in front of your siblings!"

Shannon looks at her father, disappointed in his surrender

to her mother's whimsical infatuation with Father Dale's cajoling. "I'm going to Nat's house."

Shannon walks away toward her classmate, Natalie. She with her brother, Sebastian, are waiting by her family's car to recount the scandal Tommy just caused.

Frank, with his son and youngest daughter, enters the family station wagon. The family drives away from the Church. Grace sits alone in the backseat, watching as her mother walks with Father Dale into the rectory building with the basket Liliane prepared for their private lunch. This Sunday Lunch after Mass has become a ritual that isn't to be challenged or questioned.

The drive home from the church weighs heavily on Frank's mind. There was a time when he was Liliane's hero; where did things go wrong? He recalls the conversation he and Liliane had with Father Dale as the newly stationed priest in his Rectory office, four years ago...

~ 4 ~

MARRIAGE COUNSELLING

Four years prior, husband, Frank and wife, Liliane are waiting in a living room area of their Parish Rectory for Catholic Marriage counselling from their new charismatic priest.

The Parish Secretary, Vicki Bergeron, enters the waiting area with a tray of tea and biscuits. As Frank and Liliane sit with each other, the question of why either of them lacks the inner authority to consult their conscience as a guide to understanding themselves and each other is galaxies away from their comprehension.

"Good morning, Mr. and Mrs. Bailey. I am humbled you have decided to seek my counsel. Father Edmund spoke highly of your devotion to the Church. And I was pleased to learn you both made Cursillo!" Father Dale is a charming and polite middle-aged man. He is slender, athletic, and maintains an upright posture. Almost as though an imaginary string from the Heavens pulls to elongate his neck and spine through the crown of his head.

"Why not bring your tea?" He gestures to guide them into his office, with Liliane first and shaking Frank's hand at the frame of his office door.

Liliane responds, "Oh yes. Cursillo was life-changing." Taking her seat and looking to her husband with a smile of admiration, "Frank changed so much after his Cursillo. I had to go."

Liliane takes a sip of her tea, placing the cup delicately into its saucer.

Frank interjects, "Before I forget, pass my well wishes to Father Edmund. That I hope his health is on the mend and he's enjoying his retirement." Father Dale's elderly predecessor retired on account of health restrictions limiting his ability to perform duties.

"Certainly. How about we say a prayer? That we may have the Lord's guidance and blessing." Father Dale holds out his hands to both of their hands to pray. "Heavenly Father, that you might be here with us to guide Liliane and Frank in their marriage, family, and fertility decisions. In the name of the Father, the Son, and the Holy Spirit."

Clapping his hands together. He spins around energetically to seat himself behind his desk. "Okay. So what seems to be the issue?"

Liliane begins tentatively, "I would like to be close with Frank, but my body can't handle being pregnant again. I need his permission to get my tubes tied."

Frank, adamant, "It goes against the Catechism. It goes against the Church. I cannot in good conscience allow her to do this to our family."

Father Dale lets out a deep exhale, "Frank is correct; sterilization goes against the Catechism and Catholic teachings. Have you tried to pray about it? Have you tried other methods endorsed by the Pope? *The Rhythm Method?"* He looks at them both as though sharing a magical secret, *"The Billings method?"* They both nod.

Pausing as he looks intently to Liliane, "Liliane, you don't want another baby?"

Liliane, conceding defeat, "I have varicose veins and my nerves. Tommy was such a big baby; he just about pulled out my uterus. And my nerves, Father. I just can't handle more children or even another baby." She sighs, "Maybe if we had more room, but the kids are getting older. Teenagers are difficult; they talk back, they question, and they will criticize what we don't have and their rich friends have."

"Teenagers can see things that children aren't even aware

of," Liliane says, self-conscious. "They pick up on things and they poke and probe. I just..."

Frank, defensive over the adequacy of the home he provides, interrupts, "She's gone through other pregnancies." Liliane's eyes dart to Frank, hurt and betrayed by his words.

Picking up on the source of their marital rift, Father Dale adjusts his tone to sympathetic compassion as he bridges his gaze to Liliane. "Yes. Father Edmund mentioned, when I consulted him how best to guide you both."

"It's difficult, and yet we must have faith in ourselves and the Lord." Contemplating how to navigate, Father Dale recommends, "Why don't we set up times with each of you separately?"

Separately? The concept seemed antithetical to marital counselling. This question floated just beyond the boundaries of Frank's Catholic programming. Meanwhile, Father Dale's gentle sympathy to Liliane has her persuaded.

Providing more logic, "Where I can hear both of your private confessions and we can continue this discussion in an individualized way?" Then looking to Frank, "That way I can guide you more effectively that you may return to each other as a united husband and wife." Bringing his two hands to cup within each other.

"In the meantime, I will look more closely at the Catechism for alternatives that the Holy See allows for Catholics, to help in the bedroom." He playfully winks at Liliane.

"Liliane, how does Thursday afternoon suit you? While the kids are still in school?" Liliane's heart softens at Father Dale's considerate and thoughtful choice of timing. She replies, "Yes. They are back at three and I can have a babysitter for Grace."

The Priest continues, "I'm optimistic that we will only need a couple of sessions to work this out." Elongating his posture while smiling and looking at both of them. "How about we close with a prayer?" He places his hands together and closes his eyes, proceeding to pray an elegant request for the Lord's Intervention from his infinite wisdom, to reveal what His Will is for Frank and Liliane.

As they left, Frank was experiencing a nagging feeling in his gut similar to the occasions when signing a contract with a lawyer, car salesman, realtor, or insurance broker. Compelled to take their word in good faith but an unease about navigating unfamiliar territory with this otherwise convincing Father Dale.

~ 5 ~

BODILY AUTONOMY

Liliane is fixing her lipstick, waiting for the babysitter to arrive. She has laid a three-year-old Grace down for a nap. She is going to her first private counselling session with the new parish priest, Father Dale.

Pulling out her car keys, she inspects the contents of her purse; making sure she has brought along her book, *The Thorn Birds*. A forbidden love story she bought as an escape, indulging in the appeal of an attractive, sympathetic Priest married to God.

The babysitter is a neighbour she can see walking toward the house, Liliane comes to greet her. She lets her know Grace is having her nap and that she should be home in time for when the older kids, Shannon and Tommy are back from school.

Merci Madame Bailey.

À tantôt! Au revoir!

She gets into her car. Waving good-bye to her babysitter before reversing out of the driveway. Arriving to the Rectory, she parks. Liliane looks at her lipstick in the rear view mirror. She steps out of the car, closing its door and walks up to the front entrance. Anticipating an important shift in her marriage, *this will change things.*

Vicki Bergeron, the Rectory Secretary, has been watching Liliane from the window and opens the door to greet her.

"Hello Liliane. Beautiful weather, don't you think?" Vicki forcing a welcoming voice through a locked-in-place grin at odds with the watchful vacancy in her eyes.

"A little hot for me, Vicki! You must want to get home to soak up the sun by your big in-ground pool?" Liliane's relationship to the heat is complicated by her need to compress and conceal her varicose veins wearing thick beige panty hose and long skirts. A tight, sticky reminder of an unsightly physical imperfection.

"Oh, I'll be here for a bit. I still have a few letters to type."

Coming out of his Office, Father Dale differs, "Vicki, Thank you. Those letters can be typed tomorrow and mailed out at the end of the day."

Vicki offers, "Father, I don't mind. I can finish up today."

Liliane pleading telepathically, *Oh please go.*

"I insist," he gestures his hand to guide her home. Dissembling Vicki's voyeuristic craving for more details into Liliane's strange and tragic story. "Well, you're the boss. At the risk of appearing indulgent, we spoiled ourselves with cushioned reclining lounge chairs for the pool deck." Vicki touches Liliane's forearm and adds, "Lily, we must have you and Frank over for tea. Bob has a new insurance package that covers everything. He can speak to Frank about the added benefits." There's a sales pitchy uptalk in her voice. Swept up by the spirit of Christian fellowship, Frank had already succumbed to purchasing their car, house and life insurance policies from the Bergerons, leaving Liliane to wonder *What more could they sign up for?*

Vicki sorts a few piles on her desk. Grabs her purse, wraps a scarf around her head, and exits the rectory. Waving goodbye. Glancing back from her car curiously as she pulls away.

Father Dale, striving to alleviate Liliane's tension, "I hope the added privacy can put you at ease to freely discuss. Without any snoopy ears to listen in!"

Soothed by his thoughtful courtesy, Liliane felt a rush of warmth rise to her cheeks."Yes Father. Thank you," she replied, momentarily meeting his gaze before quickly averting her eyes. Recomposing herself, "Before we begin, can I use your washroom?" When her nerves tighten up, she has to pee every so often with repeated visits to the washroom. If only she could just relax.

"I'm afraid the main washroom is out of order. You'll have to use my personal washroom if that's okay? It is through here." He leads her down a hallway into his private sleeping quarters. Pointing, "It's just in the corner. I will wait for you in my office."

Liliane looks around. The wall of his bedroom, behind a single bed and armchair, is an end to end bookshelf stacked with books of all kinds. A large section is devoted to joke books. *Jokes for all occasions, Jokes, Jokes, Jokes* and book titles on the study of *Graphology, Psychology, Mountaineering, Skiing, Hiking Guides, Sailing, Aviation*...and even *Hypnosis*.

Oddly, for a middle-aged man, the adjacent wall shelving overflows with a hoarder's collection of Teddy Bears, stuffed animals, and toys squished to precariously fill the unit sections. Liliane imagines the priest ministering to sickly children in hospitals and giving them a stuffy.

The small washroom was an exhibit of minimum personal grooming. A single green bar of soap, a bottle of Head and Shoulders anti-dandruff shampoo in the shower, a butterfly metal razor, a soap lather brush, and an overused toothbrush with worn bristles with a tightly rolled up tube of toothpaste.

Liliane finishes and walks to Father Dale's study to sit down across from him as he is seated behind his desk. The back wall behind his large wood desk is filled with religious books. Various versions of the Bible and volumes of Catechism books. Catholic-focused education manuals, titles on the lives of Saints. Other titles like *A Catholic Marriage, Ask your Husband, What would Mary Do?, Marriage Counselling in the Roman Catholic Church, The Art of Natural Family Planning* by John F. Kippley and Sheila K. Kippley, *The Act of Marriage: The Beauty of Sexual Love* by Tim LaHaye and Beverly LaHaye, *And the Two Shall Become One Flesh: A Study of Traditions in Ephesians 5:21-33* by Andrew T. Lincoln.

As Liliane sits down, "You have so many stuffed animals. Are these for children you minister?"

"No. They're mine. Gifts to me." His revelation confuses Liliane. Something is missing. *What would a grown man need by holding onto so many toys and clutter?*

He says, "I don't think anyone will come, but let me close the door." Returning to his desk, Father Dale lifts his hands to pray and closes his eyes. With a sincere and tender voice he begins, "Lord, I am here today to guide your lovely daughter, Liliane, a mother and wife among your flock. May your merciful wisdom be with us this afternoon. In the name of the Father, the Son, and the Holy Spirit. Amen."

"Amen," Liliane repeats. Her longing to have experienced a father calling her his lovely daughter is invoked within her.

Liliane, apologetic, speaks, "Father, I hope I didn't give the impression that I don't love children. It's just that my thoughts overcrowd my mind sometimes for everything that I need to look after. It's a daily battle of chaos trying to keep things clean and orderly. I can't imagine looking after another baby."

Father Dale asks bluntly, "Liliane, who told you that you need your husband's permission to get a Tubal Ligation?"

"Frank and our Family Doctor. It's always been that way."

Father Dale sighs with frustration, "As of 1968, the Province of Quebec passed Bill 42 granting women bodily autonomy for all medical procedures including Tubal Ligation. The Catholic Church discourages this procedure as it goes against God's natural plan. But the State's position is that it is *your body*."

Struck by his emphasis, Liliane protests, "How come I don't know this? Why are they saying I can't without my husband's permission?"

Father Dale, providing the benefit of the doubt, "They might not be aware of the change or they may be ignoring it. And there are men, husbands who do not want women to get ideas in their head that challenge their authority. But let's first assume they both were unaware of the change. Is your Family Doctor Catholic?"

Liliane replies, "He's Anglican." Stunned by this revelation, she continues, "I'm upset about this. It's always like that, not letting a woman know what might impact her. But then I am supposed to offer an account of every detail of my life, like a child? My sins, my shortcomings and every fuckin' decision or purchase, OOPS!" Covering her mouth. "Pardon me. I have to explain and defend everything. Always a full audit on the merit of my virtue as a mother and wife."

"In a marriage, transparency and being in agreement with each other is vital to have a happy home life. No matter what religion," he offers pragmatically, recalling Frank's inflexibility on Liliane's wishes.

A storm has ignited inside her. Liliane is now disinhibited, "Father, I can't agree with you more. I give everything and then he half shares so that he can maintain the illusion of HIS piety. His sins and confessions are humble brags, *'I should have donated more.'* And the big one, *'I left this company when I learned they wanted to make weapons for war.'* You hear what I am saying? The confession is a pat on the back, to emphasize how holy he is." Liliane shakes her head.

"Tsk. Father, do you see where things are at in my Marriage? Transparency? He would have known about this Bill 42. He stays on top of every change because he believes we are nearing the End Days. *HE KNEW!"*

Father Dale allows for a moment of silence as Liliane reflects on her situation. He broaches the subject, "Liliane, can you tell me about the times you were pregnant? Can you recount your first experience?"

She bursts into tears. "Father, I have already confessed my sins. If I must keep confessing the same sin, and each time beating myself up while telling another person, then when am I forgiven? When am I free?"

Father Dale reassures her, "I am not asking for your confession. I would just like to understand you better."

Liliane recalls her first experience as a mother, where two nuns and a priest have convinced her that the most generous and loving thing she could do was let go of her daughter as she was a single mother and without the means to provide. She remembers her younger self, signing a document while crying. Then having just one last Good Bye with her two-year-old daughter. Unbeknownst to her, the Church was selling children to infertile couples. A tragedy and regret that continues its turn like a broken wheel, repeatedly hitting against the sides of Liliane's mind.

Father Dale moves closer to her to provide her a tissue. Endearingly, he says "Lily, you were freed when Christ offered his body on the cross. That selfless act was to pay the ransom for your sins and for my sins too."

Liliane, sobbing profoundly, is comforted by his tenderness and patience, "I don't feel free. I didn't know I had the right to *Bodily Autonomy*. I need to think about what that means? Bodily Autonomy. It sounds like ownership and control. Something I haven't ever felt I had. I'm 42 years old. I have given Frank 3 healthy, smart children. Each of them has two arms and two legs, and they are healthy. They are beautiful. Three is enough!"

Father Dale gets up and retrieves a book from the shelf behind him. He reads the title, *The Art of Natural Family Planning!* Brings it to Liliane and sits on the edge of his desk. Looking at her with a notable intrigue.

He asks, "Have you a copy of this book?" He hands her the book and continues, "The Catechism is clear that a Tubal Ligation is against the Vatican's teachings. Perhaps we can pray that the Lord speaks to your's and Frank's heart in the coming weeks? Providing insight into His plan for you as a couple and family."

Liliane looking down at the book's cover acknowledges, "Frank has always been loving to me when I have been pregnant."

Pleading she says, "It's just not physically in me to do it again. And God Bless the women who mother children with 'issues', I admire them. I am not one of them. I'm on tranquilizers for the children I have. God help me! Father, I am not a Saint. And Tommy? When he isn't drawing or painting, he's so naughty!"

She proclaims, "You can't push a woman into taking on more than is in her heart. Even the Virgin Mary had only one kid!"

In agreement, "True. One wonderful Son." Taking another pause for emphasis, "Liliane, what would Jesus tell you? Pray upon that. What would Mary tell you?"

"The other women my age, their husbands brought them to have the procedure when their wives decided. And I know this to be the case for some Catholics." Liliane resisting her impulse to gossip, holds back their names on the tip of her tongue.

"Yes. My duty is to listen, try to bring sense to the challenges that God places before us, and guide you in the teach-

ings of the Catholic Church. What others are doing, if their influence leads you to sin against God's Plan..."
Interrupting, "Father, I'm going to go to Hell if I get my tubes tied?"

"Surely not!" Father Dale concurs. "Well, I will be in Hell if I have to have another baby at this age and living in that tiny house. If it's too much on me, I might be driven to do something that guarantees my place in Hell."

Encouraging her, "Give yourself some time. Follow the recommendations in that book. They might help. After all you have been through, Lily, whatever you decide to do, it is your body, your conscience, and your soul. If you wait, eventually a woman's fertility window closes. If you can be patient, knowing God has thought of everything."

Liliane is amused, "You mean Menopause? Can you ask Frank to wait for my Menopause?" Reflecting the notion and imposition on Frank's piety. She begins laughing to herself, while wiping her nose with a squished tissue. Refreshed by this new suggestion, "Father, we should have you over for dinner. With the whole family."

Father Dale agrees, "That would be lovely, Lily...Liliane. Let us do that after I have met with Frank privately."

Liliane drives off from the rectory. On her way home, she turns into the McDonald's drive-through. Approaching the intercom to place her menu order, a teenage voice crackled through the intercom, *"Je peux prendre votre commande?"*

Speaking into the box while scanning the large billboard of menu items, *"Oui, je vais prendre un Big Mac, des frites moyen format, un chausson aux pommes, 4 morceaux de Poulet mcCroquettes, une boisson grand format de Coca, et uhm, et uhm. Ouais, bin c'est tout. Merci."*

She rolls to a stop to pay at the first window and then collects her order at the next. The girl in uniform says innocently with a smile leaning over delivering her order, *"Bon Appetit, Madame."*

"Merci." Liliane retrieves the brown hot bag of styrofoam packaging and steamy aroma, placing it on the passenger seat beside her.

Not yet ready to go home, she drives the family Station Wagon to a Park overlooking the river. Sitting there alone at a picnic bench, contemplating her exchange with Father Dale. She can't help but emotionally eat 'stuffing her feelings'. The perfect thin French fries, dunking *les mcCroquettes* into the sweet and sour sauce and eating too quickly half of the Big Mac. Going over her conversations with Frank, with her doctor and mumbling the words *bodily autonomy* to herself, shaking her head.

Taking a sip of Coca Cola, she decides to read her book. Pulling it out of her purse. She's at the part where Father Ralph takes Meggie in to live with him, after he discovers that she's being harshly mistreated by Sister Agatha. Beating her with a paddle for biting her nails. If only there was someone who would have done the same for Lily when she was raised by the nuns. Finishing her *chausson aux pommes* she accepts it's time to make her way home. Throwing away the McDonald's bags and leftovers in the park's trash bin, Liliane get's back into the family station wagon.

Arriving just in time to pay the baby sitter, who's been looking after 3 year old Grace as Shannon and Tommy return home from school.

Delegating babysitting to Shannon. "Shannon, can you look after Grace? Let her play in your room while you do your homework. Mummy needs some alone time."

Shannon asks, "What's for dinner?"

"There's a lasagna you can take out of the fridge for when your father comes home. I just need some quiet," Liliane says, walking away to her bedroom.

"Mom, is everything alright?" Shannon calls out to her. "I don't know," Liliane replies before closing her door behind.

She rushes to her washroom toilet and makes herself throw up all the junk food she just ingested. It comes up in the reverse stream of her ruminations. Thinking *I hate McDonald's.*

Brushing her teeth, and rinsing her mouth with mouthwash. She looks back at her reflection, mustering a conviction to make a phone call.

"Hi Barbara, it's Lily. Is this a good time? I need to ask you something private." Barb is one of Liliane's better friends. Non-judgemental, funny, and supportive.

"Just a minute, Lil', Let me change phones," Barb responds, before asking her sons to hang up the line when she tells them to. She walks to a more private setting, picking up the phone and calling out, "I got it! Boys, you can hang up!" Her boys in the kitchen hang up the phone to make the click. Then one gently pulls the receiver off the hook to eavesdrop on their mom's call.

"Hi Barb, Can I ask you the name of your lady doctor? I would like to see her, " Liliane confides.

"Her name is Dr. Leblanc." Opening her phone book, "Her number is 514-234-5555. She's wonderful. I just gave her name to a friend who told me Dr. Thompson suggested the way for her to fix her migraines and mood was to have more sex. Then he volunteered himself, and would you believe, in the most disgusting way!" Barb laughed.

Liliane responds, "I thought he was a good doctor but I had no one to compare him to. Thank you, Barbara. So that's 5-1-4-2-3-4-5-5-5-5?"

Barbara confirms, "That's it. I hope everything is okay and you are in good health?"

"Yes. Good-bye Barbara, Thanks again." Liliane says in a quiet voice. Reserving her thoughts to herself.

"Bye Liliane. I'll see you on Sunday! God Bless." They each hang up the phone. Liliane reaches for the book given to her by Father Dale. Sifting through the pages to review the 'recommendations' in small doses. She sets the book on Frank's bedside table. Pulling instead for her novel, *The Thorn Birds*. She fantasizes, imagining Father Dale on a thoroughbred horseback as Father Ralph de Bricassart.

Frank walks in with his suit from his day at work. With some concern, he asks, "Shannon is preparing dinner. Are you unwell?"

"I feel sick to my stomach, " she looks at him before asking him sincerely, "Frank, do you want another baby?"

He answers, " I want to follow the Church's teachings. Is that why you're sick?"

"Frank, where will the baby sleep when they grow up? If I get pregnant, will we have a bigger house?" To Liliane, this seems like a reasonable negotiation of terms.

Frank declares, "We have plenty of room! The children can share their rooms! You can try to be a better mother. More loving..."

Liliane, a flood of tears follow after her words, "You are saying I am a bad mother? You know how that hurts me. You know *why* that hurts me!" Liliane has a sharp flashback of holding her first-born daughter for the very last time.

In the kitchen, a three-year-old Grace interprets for Shannon what she has overheard, "They're fighting about babies. She doesn't like them."

Shannon has been watching Tommy jerk about like an imbecile break dancing and answers, "She's had enough. Especially with Tommy and the nightmare he's turning out to be."

~ 6 ~

WOMEN'S CURSILLO

Earlier that afternoon, Vicki Bergeron returns home to tend to her lush flower garden that surrounds the perimeter of her pool. Her sister, Wanda who lives down the block is over for a swim. Her garden is a colourful arrangement of purple pop-pop alliums, big orange tiger lilies, daisies, and climbing vines with pink trumpet flowers that scale the back fence.

Gossiping freely that Frank and Liliane have begun marriage counselling with Father Dale, Vicki recounts Liliane's testimony at the Women's Cursillo retreat years prior. "Strict confidence, Wanda. Not a word to anyone you heard from me. But let me tell you this poor woman has no concept of who to tell what."

Wanda is doing her breast stroke, attentively listening to her sister betray Liliane's misplaced confidence. Wanda an independent active woman. Only on occasion attends mass with her adult children for social connection to other anglophones.

Vicki describes an overnight Women's Retreat in the Laurentian Mountains. She elaborates upon one of these days, where the attendees are to participate in a cleansing from their sins by sharing their 'testimony'. A hippyish Kool-Aid vibe is set by this musician woman, Janet. She leads the women in song, playing her guitar. Vicki continues, "We're in this rustic Chapel with pane less windows, holding hands, singing some Nana Mouskouri song, how's it go?" Vicki pauses, seeking the melody. "Anyway, this woman tells us, *God doesn't want you to be stuck in your sin. He wants you to find healing and step into the incredible life that he has for you. In the Gospel, it says, 'Confess your sins to one another and pray for one another, that you may be healed. '* She invites Liliane to go first!" Wanda is shaking her head.

"Entering the circle, Liliane provides her testimony, *Hello, my name is Liliane. I had relations with a man out of wedlock and I became pregnant.* The man, a jazz musician and alcoholic left her at 6 months pregnant and after 2 years of trying to raise the baby on her own in poverty, she gives her two year old daughter up for adoption! Wanda, Can you believe it?" Vicki now convinced of her talent for story telling by borrowing the drama of Liliane's life.

"So you know, she had no measure of how deep to dive! Good Heavens! It was so disturbing. She was crying and upset. God help her!" Vicki rolling her eyes, feigning as much compassion that her vanity permitted as she pulled the weeds from her garden.

Vicki concludes with hindsight, "Hers was not a true confession. Just a tiresome plea for sympathy." Standing up to wipe her garden gloves on her apron, she exclaimed, "*Dec Colores!* That was the song." Relishing her moment of triumphant recall.

~ 7 ~

FALSE PROPHET

It's after school, Tommy has ventured into the woods with a mission. Teetering beyond, adolescent defiance, he and his squad are crouched behind bushes. Him with his army beret, his comrades in Rambo bandanas. Their faces all streaked with camouflage paint, and they're dressed in army garbs. They are staking out a home construction site. Listening in and waiting for cues as workers pack up to leave after a full day's work.

As the 'enemy' trucks pull away, they listen for the sounds of voices or footsteps within the frame of the house. In full militia mode, the boys signal to each other that it's their moment to invade. In their world of imagination and adventure, they were intrepid commandos on a critical supply run, not a group of delinquent thirteen-year-olds about to make a serious mistake.

Their target: stacks of lumber and plywood, a bounty of materials to build their underground fort. An invisible escape from moms and sisters, hidden deep within the woods.

Meanwhile Liliane is driving home after an annual follow-up with her new OBGYN, Dr. Leblanc. It's the third time she's seen Dr. Leblanc, since deciding to adopt a stance of personal privacy. After performing the awkward exam, Dr. Leblanc confirmed, " Mrs. Bailey, everything feels fine. Do you experience any pain during sex?" A question to which, Liliane answered, "No."

Her reply leading Dr. Leblanc to assume, "Did your husband finally come around to your decision?"

Liliane confides, "He doesn't know and has decided to wait until I go through Menopause to remain holy."

"I'm sorry to hear that. One could say a remarkable devotion to dogma on his part?" Unimpressed, Dr. Leblanc looks down to review her notes. "Mrs. Bailey, you listed a few medications prescribed by Dr. Thomson. Have you considered speaking with a psychologist ?"

Liliane replies, "Father Dale, my parish priest counsels me. He's the one who encouraged me to have my tubes tied?"

Dr. Leblanc is surprised, "Encouraged? A Catholic Priest?"

Liliane adds, "Oh he's different! He's the one who told me I didn't need my husband's permission. So I trust him."

Dr. Leblanc observes Mrs. Bailey intently. "Still, Father Dale isn't a qualified or registered Psychotherapist that understands the effects of these drugs. I am going to write down for you three names of experts that I encourage you to consult. I believe it is in your interest to get off these tranquilizers and prescriptions. Please, no alcohol or driving if you have taken valium."

Liliane pulls into her driveway, grateful how much meal preparation she attended to in advance for this evening's dinner guest. Father Dale will be over to critique Tommy's artwork. Entering her home through the kitchen side door, Tommy is seated on a stool at the counter in his beret and army garbs. He is dipping chocolate chip cookies and drinking a large glass of milk.

Liliane says, "Oh Tommy what on earth are you wearing? You're all dirty! You're going to spoil your dinner eating so many cookies!" Seeing him dunk his cookie in his milk, with war paint on his face highlighted how much he was still just a kid playing in an imaginary world. Still Father Dale was coming.

Adjusting her tone to exude patience, Liliane says, "Tommy, get cleaned up and prepare your painting to show Father Dale. You can set it up in the living room."

Liliane begins preparing dinner, placing casserole dishes in the oven. Just as her mother calls out, "Shannon, Father Dale is coming for dinner. Can you help me by setting the table?" Shannon enters the kitchen, startling her mom.

Shannon asks, "What are we eating?"

Her mum replies, "Breaded chicken with broccoli and potatoes. For dessert, cherry pie with ice cream."

"Can I make a salad?"

Liliane replies, "Yes, that would be nice."

Shannon gathers the ingredients: cucumber, tomatoes, red onion, Boston lettuce from the fridge setting them upon the island counter. Then grabbing for the Salad bowl, cutting board, and knife from the drawers, she tentatively asks her mother, "Mom, do you have any friends who aren't Catholic?"

Liliane looks up drawing a blank. Quebec was predominantly French and Catholic. She answers uncertain, "It feels like we do, but I can't think of any right now."

Shannon ventures to ask, "What art training does Father Dale have to critique Tommy's work?"

"Oh gosh Shannon! Father Dale has been to Rome! To the Vatican. He's seen the Sistine Chapel! He's seen all the works by da Vinci, Michelangelo... I can't remember all the names. That's more that can be said for that 'art' teacher at your school."

Shannon challenges, "You mean the art teacher with a Master's in Fine Arts studies from France ? And the one with an exhibit at the Art Gallery across from the *Museé des Beaux Arts*?"

Liliane doubting her daughter's claim, "Is that so? I'll have to ask Dale about that."

Frank enters the kitchen by the back door. Arriving home from his day at work as an Electric Engineer. A photograph of the Pope is behind him on the Wall. He greets his wife and daughter, "Hello. We'll say the rosary after dinner?"

Shannon pleads, "Oh please Dad. We just said the rosary on Saturday. We couldn't watch Star Wars unless." Overwhelmed by the news and increasing conflicts between the US and USSR Frank copes with his apocalyptic anxieties by getting his children to pray the full rosary.

In this ceremony, the family is seated around the dining room table holding hands. Frank earnestly prays the Hail Mary with his eyes closed. Tommy and Shannon make faces at each other from across the table. Tommy squeezes his sister Grace's fingers to make her cry. Frank doing his utmost to ignore their behaviour, closing his eyes to stay in prayer. Liliane tries to keep the children under control with disapproving glances and gestures. By the third or fourth decade, Frank all of a sudden loses his patience, *Shhhh-shing* loudly and squeezing Shannon and Tommy's hands to urge their focus. Liliane, finding herself giggle at Frank's frustration.

Perhaps on edge about hosting yet another dinner with his confessor, Frank raises his voice with alarm, " With the world on the brink of Nuclear Apocalypse, the least we can do is say the rosary for World Peace before we eat dessert!"

Liliane responds, "Not tonight Frank. Can we lighten the mood? Tommy is showing Dale his art." There it was, she dropped the title 'Father', referring to him as Dale. Taking the salad Shannon's prepared she says, "Thank you, Shannon. Can you play some music for us? "Für Elise" or "Clair de Lune"?"

Usually, Shannon's piano playing was a soothing remedy for Liliane's nerves and a source of pride. After four years of lessons, Shannon was able to shift her mother's state instantly. If she started playing either of these two songs, her mom was subdued. If those weren't enough, "Pachelbel's Canon in D Major" proved the ultimate pacifier.

In the background, Shannon could hear her parents bicker over the family ceremony of saying the rosary. A proxy argument for something more pernicious.

Liliane saying to Frank, "You expect your children to exonerate your past deeds by saying the rosary with you?"

"Yes. Exactly. It's critical and our only hope!" Frank pleads with Liliane.

Before returning to his faith, as a lapsed Catholic he took his most high-paying job at Boeing Missile Defence. While celebrated by his colleagues for further enhancing the efficiency of ICBM nuclear missiles, Frank confronted by a crisis of conscience, fanatically returned to Catholicism. Developing an obsessive-compulsive trait of evaluating every misstep, temptation, deed, or bad thought. Eschewing the pursuit of economic success beyond basic necessities, as it most surely would lead to eternal damnation.

Overhearing his mother and father, Tommy arrives in the kitchen to bestow his blessing. Putting his arms up, imitating a Priest singing a sermon. *"Heavenly Father have mercy on us and forgive us our many, many sins and failings. We all need to pray for World Peace. The balance between good and evil is determined by our unity in prayer. Then we can all indulge freely in Cherry Pie and ice cream.*" Liliane can't help laughing and Frank not so much.

The doorbell rings. Shannon stops her Piano playing abruptly to close the key lid.

While Liliane rushes to greet Father Dale at the door and guide him into the living room. Tommy sets up an easel in the living room, returning with a covered canvas.

When everyone has arrived and their eyes are turned toward him, Tommy boldly unveils his canvas. It's a detailed oil outline of a nude woman (Mary Magdalene) on the cross and Jesus at her feet. Confidently he points, "That's Mary Magdalene and this is Jesus."

Frank, Liliane, and Father Dale are a gasp at the work.

Tommy asserts with adamant conviction, "It's my painting. I get to choose what I PAINT."

Frank asks, "Did your art teacher put you up to this?"

Shannon says, "I think it's excellent!"

Liliane appalled, "Jesus, worshipping a nude woman? A prostitute, Shannon!

Shannon says, "No. It's a role reversal, like the washing of the feet. It's genius, Tommy!" Tommy smiles and agrees.

Father Dale is moving in closer to inspect, holding his fingers to his chin, "Interesting observation Shannon. Is this acrylic, Tommy?"

Tommy replies confidently, "Oil."

Father Dale finds himself at a loss for input or technical suggestions as the painting's subject rendering are remarkably advanced for a thirteen-year-old. He awkwardly suggests, "Tommy, have you considered putting something in this corner, it's a bit empty? Maybe you could cover her with something, a cloth or robe?"

Baffled by the suggestion, Tommy replies, "What? She has to be naked! That's the point!"

Liliane flustered and blushing, "Dinner's ready! Let's all go to the dining room." The family and their dinner guest move into the dining room.

"On a lighter note, I have a story." Father Dale proceeds to begin a story. Father Dale sits at the head of the table across from Frank. The priest goes on to share a series of jokes and stories that he laughs at with Liliane seated at his left, doting on him.

The main meal draws to an end. Liliane is out of breath from her laughing. She places her hand on Father Dale's forearm, "Dale, How do you come up with these stories?"

Shannon is beside her and exasperated by her mother's fawning. She asks, "Can I be excused?"

Frank says, " We have a guest." Liliane has gotten up to clear the plates and bring the dessert.

Shannon says, "I have my bursary and scholarship applications to complete and an exam to study for." Liliane says, "Shannon, help me clear the table, you too Grace. Then I will bring dessert. "

Grace asks Shannon, "Can I study with you?" Shannon tells her, "I'm sorry Grace. I will need to focus."

Tommy teases, "You have nothing to study for."

Shannon clears the last of the plates and butter dish. Tommy asks, "Was that real butter?"

Frank annoyed, "Would you ask that if you were invited to the Queen's table?"

Tommy chirping back, "Would you serve margarine, if you were hosting the Queen?"

In an effort to conceal an adversarial tension, Father Dale asks, "How's your work, Frank?"

Aware that his wife has been confiding all her frustrations without discretion. Frank replies with minimum, "Good."

"Here's dessert!" Liliane and Grace return to the table with dessert plates. Grace gives one to her father and brother. Liliane serves Father Dale and sits down beside him, looking over at Frank.

Shannon now in her room is at her desk. She is going through School pamphlets and a book that lists all the different scholarships and bursary categories available to her in order to attend and board at a private Cégep when she completes her Secondary V.

There's a knock at her door. It's Tommy. He's come in imitating Father Dale's voice, knocking with the door slightly open, *"Hi, it's me Father Dale. Can I help you with your letters?"* He continues in a weird whisper, as though secretly intruding on Shannon's space, *"I went to School. I'm an expert at letters!"* The fact he's making fun of the house guest just in the other room, makes Shannon burst into hysterics.

Shannon laughing through the tension, "He's such a weirdo! I can't believe what you painted! It was amazing. Did you see mom's face?"

"Of course!" Tommy celebrating his artistic rebellion.

Tommy asks Shannon, "Do you think Dad wants him over?"

"I don't know. I don't understand." There's a knock at the door. It's Grace, she's heard them laughing and has opened the door to join on their fun. "Can I come in?"

Shannon gestures her to enter saying, "Just for a minute."

Grace whispers, "They're in the living room and mom's sitting right beside Father Dale and complaining to dad about Tommy's painting."

In the living room, Frank seeks to expose Father Dale's depth of knowledge in the fine arts. "What do you make of Dali's work?"

Father Dale, "I haven't heard of him."

Liliane chiming in, "Frank, are you an art critic now?"

Frank points to Tommy's canvas, "He's painted just like Dali. Salvador Dali? *St. John of the Cross?* And his *Crucifixion?*"

Liliane is becoming irritated, "Are you trying to make me feel stupid? After your son paints a nude prostitute?" She emphasizes, looking to Dale and back to Frank, "A prostitute, Frank!"

Unwilling to conceal her contempt, Liliane is glaring at Frank with a conspirator's smirk of knowing. For Father Dale has broken the sacred seal of her husband's confession extracted from him during private marriage counselling.

The subtext of Liliane's insinuation has not escaped Frank. He advocates, "He painted *Mary Magdalene* who repented of her sins. Liliane, you are too critical of our son." He looks over to Father Dale attempting to perceive the extent that he has been betrayed.

Under his gaze, Father Dale quickly gets up to say, "It was a lovely dinner and I look forward to the next time. Tommy is talented. I wish I could say his painting will keep him out of trouble." He looks at the canvas one more time, then says, "He's unlikely to skirt controversy with this." As he points to the painting.

Frank escorts Father Dale to the door, questioning if his paranoia has been triggered by the raw intensity of Tommy's painting of Mary Magdalene and all that she represents.

Observing Father Dale walk away and into his get-away car, only to witness Liliane chase after him with a dessert plate covered with aluminum foil. From inside, Frank holds the front door open for his wife as she says another good-bye to Father Dale.

As she returns up their driveway, Frank watchfully reflects upon the disclosures he believed were made in absolute confidence to his Priest.

Once Liliane crosses their door frame, Frank closes the door behind them. Telling her, " I'll clean up and put away all the dishes."

With a hint of remorse for her earlier behavior, she replies, "Thank you, Frank."

Washing dishes after dinner serves as a meditative activity for Frank. He reexamines the single private marriage counselling session that he had with Father Dale.

Frank is seated across from Father Dale. At first Father Dale's question seemed benign, Frank believing these to put his mind at ease and gently break the ice on the stale-mate between he and Liliane.

"Frank, you were intimate with a woman before Liliane?" Father Dale asks carefully. "Was there more than one?"

Frank, " I confess Father, there was more than one."

Father Dale, "You loved these women? The way you love your wife?"

Frank, uncomfortable confides, "No, I regret I did not love these women as I love my wife. The first of these was my first time. I was like many young men, wanting to have experience from a woman who was an expert in that regard."

Father Dale asks, "Ah a woman of the night? Have you confessed these exchanges to Liliane?"

"No, that was before her and I confessed and repented when I came back to my faith."
Father Dale says, "Liliane does not believe she will be a good mother to another child."

Frank responding, "Well, she has said as much. Her nerves and her past."

"Frank, children and a wife require strong leadership in the husband and father. What can I do to help you be a better husband to Liliane?"

Frank asks, "How do you mean?"

Father Dale treads carefully, "It's a delicate subject. Father Edmund mentioned your testimony in the men's group of Cursillo." Frank becomes tense, and defensive. Feeling the thorns of his confession being made to prick back at him.

Father Dale explains, "With your consent, I will need to see Liliane more often on her own. I'd like to counsel her, to help her forgive herself."

"Given what you have confessed today and in Cursillo, I suggest a suitable penance for you is to wait until Liliane has gone through Menopause before you have relations with her. That is my best recommendation for you to meet the guidance by Our Holy See and the Catechism."

"That could be twelve years from now!" Frank said, astonished at the recommendation.

"Frank, I know your past weighs heavily on your conscience. Offer this sacrifice as penance. Then I may absolve you of all your sins," Father Dale advises, "Now let us close with a prayer."

And just like that, with a plate slipping through his hands to shatter across the floor, Frank realized what he agreed to.

~ 8 ~

THE THORN BIRDS

Liliane's novel, *The Thorn Birds* has been adapted into a made for TV series. As she has been doing for each evening the mini series has aired, Liliane has popped popcorn and melted butter for her, Tommy and Shannon to share while watching while Frank catches up on bills and letters from the study. In her pyjamas, Grace is lying on the carpet watching the series with a small bowl of popcorn until her bedtime.

The deep and dramatic TV voice...BRYAN BROWN, RACHEL WARD AND RICHARD CHAMBERLAIN - A LOVE UNATTAINABLE, FORBIDDEN, FOREVER. THE THORN BIRDS. Followed by the upbeat, score by Henry Mancini.

As the scenes become increasingly mature, Liliane tells Grace, "Grace, time for bed." Grace slowly gets up walking backward watching as much more content as she can, lingering sneakily behind the family room entry to watch the scene develop of the Priest and Meggie having an affair on the beach. Grace can't help but let out a giggle.

"I said, Get to bed!" Liliane annoyed that this intense moment of forbidden romance had been spoiled.

Grace perceiving not to irritate her mother further, brings herself to bed. On her way, she says a good night to Cana, who is lying at her father's feet, giving him a hug and kiss good night. "Good night, Daddy." He answers, "Good night, Grace. Sweet dreams. Say your prayers."

Once laying her head down on her pillow, she almost immediately falls asleep. But not before reciting the framed prayer on her wall, *"Now I lay me down to sleep, I pray the Lord my soul to keep, if I should die before I wake, I pray the Lord my soul to take."*

Grace then enters the dimension of her subconscious. She is kneeling before a statue of the Virgin Mary praying and the Church has caught fire and flames are all around her though she doesn't feel fear or the heat. Before her eyes, the statue of Mary is melting, and emerging from the core is a living version of Mary herself in the flesh.

Reaching for Mary's hand, saying, "Mary, I will show you the way out." Grace hold's the Virgin Mother's gentle hand for a second and feels an outpouring of maternal love before her own mother, Liliane appears to slap her hand away. "You're not to touch her!" Liliane snaps. Grace previously unafraid, is flooded with shame. The three of them are now fleeing the structure with flames all around them. Grace wakes up crying.

Frank walks in to check on her crying, "Is everything okay?" He asks while sitting by her on the bedside. "You were screaming. Do you remember what was troubling you?"

Grace tells him crying, "The Church was burning and the statue of Mary was melting." Cana is licking the salt from her tears. Grace lifts her blanket tapping her bed, "Can Cana sleep with me." Cana has jumped in and rolled up beside her. Frank unable to say no, " This one time." He kisses her on her forehead. Slightly concerned by the symbolic nature of his daughter's nightmare.

In the living room the final scene of The Thorn Birds saga is coming to a conclusion. Liliane is sobbing. Her teenage children are rolling their eyes to each other, all too aware the parallel meaning the series represents to their mother.

The next morning over breakfast, Grace tells her mother about the dream she had. Omitting the part where Liliane slaps her hand away from Mary.

"I had a dream nightmare. I was at Church and all the walls were burning around me. The statue of Mary was melting but as the statue melted, the real Mary appeared.

I went to hold her hand and show her the way out of the Church."

Liliane astounded, "Did Mary say anything to you in this dream? Like a message?"

Grace answers, "No."

Liliane can't help but interpret the dream as a prophetic sign that her daughter was sharing. "Father Dale should hear this! I'm going to tell him all about it. My little daughter having such a dream. I wonder what it means? He will be riveted. Grace, your dream could be hinting at something, like the Children of Fatima!"

Liliane continues intensely, "Grace, now this is very important. On Thursday, you go to your friend Sophie's house after school. Father Dale will be visiting and it's better you aren't here. We need it quiet."

Grace pleads with her mother, not understanding how her mother's attention always shifts away from her to Father Dale, "But I can be quiet. I will just stay downstairs until he leaves."

"No. That won't do. Also about the kids at school. Don't mention Father Dale comes to our house. You know our family is close with Father Dale and he really loves all of us so much. Your friend's could get jealous because he's so special and important. Don't let any of them know he visits okay? They won't understand why he visits. It's not fair to them. He's really important and he just can't be as close as he is with us, with everyone."

Liliane's arrangements to spend time with Father Dale increasingly begin to pose an inconvenience. Father Dale serves as the Chaplain at Grace's Catholic School. Grace already ashamed of her mother's addictive obsession to this man, has to now pretend that she doesn't know him when he visits her classroom to tell a series of jokes that she has already heard.

~ 9 ~

LISTENING SKILLS

The Teacher is performing a listening skills test. Each student is supposed to recall the story and answer A,B or C. Grace is seated at her desk drawing in her listening skills notebook. The facing pages are divided into sections for the current assessment and previous graded assessments which, in the case of Grace's workbook are full of red x's and evaluation scores of 3/20, 13/20, 10/20. The margins are full of Grace's drawings and doodles.

Teacher looking around to her students as she speaks with a tone of gameshow suspense, "Number 20. In today's story, Poppy was; A) competing in a swim meet B) helping her mom with dinner C) practicing her dance routine for a school talent show.

Grace looks around to her classmates for inspiration and guesses 'A'.

The three o'clock school bell rings and the kids all bring their notebooks to the teacher's desk. The children are in an uproar to get their school bags and jackets on to go home. Grace is biting her nails knowing she must coordinate an after-school play date with one of her school friends; Sophie, Carla, or Julia without appearing needy or desperate.

The teacher says, "Okay. That's it for today. Don't forget that tomorrow is gym day. Wear proper running shoes!"

Manoeuvring to approach her friend, Sophie nonchalantly. Grace says, "On Thursday, Can I come to your house after school?" Sophie replies, "I'll have to ask my mom. Phone me when you get home."

The school day is ended and Grace gets on her school bus and walks home. Grace places her schoolbag on the kitchen table. Calls Sophie's house, dialing her number on a touchpad phone. Each button has a longer sound haptic for the bigger number.

Colleen, Sophie's mum picks up the phone, "Hello?"

"Hi Colleen, it's Grace. May I speak to Sophie please?" Grace asks. Colleen calls out "Sophie it's for you, it's your friend, Grace."   The receiver is put down on the counter and Grace can hear the background noises of Sophie's mum shuffling about in the kitchen. Then Sophie picks up the phone to say, "Hello?"

Grace shyly asks, "Hi, So I was wondering is it okay if I come to your house after school on Thursday, then my mom will pick me up before dinner?"

Sophie half-heartedly, "Oh Yah, Mom can I have Grace over after school on Friday?"

Grace panicked on the other end, " No Thursday! Thursday!"

Sophie adjusts, "I mean Thursday, can Grace come over Thursday?"

Her mum replies, "Sophie, you have to do your homework after school. And Tammy cleans the house on Thursday, so having a friend over will interfere with her doing her job. The weekend is best."

Sophie speaking into the receiver to Grace, "Could you hear?"

Disappointed she replies, "Yes. The weekend instead. Okay then. I'll see you tomorrow, Sophie." Grace rubbing her brow, places the phone receiver on the hook. Bracing herself to knock on her mother's door. "Mom, I can't go to Sophie's house. It's a school night and Colleen wants Sophie to do her homework. I can just go downstairs. I will be quiet and I will be busy doing my homework."

Liliane says, "Homework? That Colleen, such a phoney."

"No. You can't be in the house. We tried that before. Dale doesn't want you here. I really need this time with Father Dale because he helps me. Don't you want me to be happy? I don't want you to hear me or us talking. I might cry and it's better you aren't here. He's such a busy man and Thursday afternoon is the only time he can come to see me."

Grace confused as to why she would want to be with someone who might make her cry, when she already sees him for her special lunch. " What about Sundays?"

Liliane interrupting with a definitive solution, "Carla. Her house is closer and I'll pick you up *after* dinner."

Deflated, Grace decides to go for a bike ride through the neighbourhood. Following her impulse to flow with the direction of the streets and her instinct, she forgets when riding a bike path through a children's park. Oh no, there they were out on their front lawn. A group of French girls are playing on their front lawn. They recognize Grace, *"Eh, t'es donc bin stupide de venir ici? T'es pas permis! Vas-t'en bloque!"* The other girls chime in, *"Ouais, vas-t'ten bloque!"* The oldest girl emboldened chases Grace on her bike. She awkwardly tries to pick up speed and the younger ones are chanting, *"Tête-carrée, tête-carrée, tête-carrée!"* Holding their two hands up by their faces to make the shape of a square head.

The older girl has run up to Grace's bike to hold on to the back metal handle of her banana bike seat. Grace pedals harder to break away from her resistance before the girl decides to let go. Yelling at her a final, *"Vas-t-en! Maudite anglaise!"* As Grace bikes away, she looks back to see her returning back with the others laughing at their triumph over their territory.

If only Grace had gone to the French primary school like Shannon and Tommy, she would have a snappy come back in French. But instead her mom decided to place her in the Catholic English school where Father Dale was the Chaplain. Grace was always delighted when her mother would drop in to say 'hello', dressed beautiful with her red lipstick framing her beautiful smile. Imperceptible to a young Grace, that her mother was in fact choreographing a random encounter with Father Dale.

The next day at school, Grace and all her classmates are to participate in the sacrament of confession with Father Dale. The class of young students is lined up outside the Chaplain's office. Grace, under pressure forces a smile, "Hey Carla, I was thinking it would be fun to come to your house on Thursday? Tomorrow?"

Carla answers, "Yah, my mom loves you. But I have to work in my father's store and you will have to help." Carla has an Italian family. Her parents immigrated after WWII.

They are loud, vibrant, and hard-working. Carla has an older brother that has been permanently injured from a car accident that has devastated the family. Carla carries the stress on her body with excess weight.

Julia interrupts, "We have to practice our confession." Standing in front of Carla, she asks her, "Carla, what are you going to say? What about you, Grace?"

Grace says, "I'll just tell him I lied about something."

Julia whispers, "He's so creepy. Confession is creepy."

Grace couldn't agree more. Overwhelmed with embarrassment by her family and her mother's association with the priest. Despite her mother's insistence she keep the relationship secret, Grace dreaded anyone knowing the truth.

"Julia, what are you going to confess?" Grace asks curiously.

Julia answers joking, "Hmmmm. I don't know yet. I will have to make something up because I am a perfect angel and I never sin." The girls laugh and poke at each other while waiting in line for their turn to have a private confession with creepy Father Dale.

Their teacher tells them, "Girls, girls. Quiet and orderly. Prayer hands. And quiet. Shhh."

When it's Grace's turn she enters Father Dale's office. The elephant in the room is looming awkwardly occupying every bit of open space.

Father Dale speaks to her, performing a make-believe 'outside this space, we don't know each other' in a patronizing unfamiliar tone, "Good morning, do you have anything to confess?"

Grace offers, "I didn't lie but I didn't tell the truth either. Someone told me that it was better I didn't tell the truth because it would hurt other people's feelings."

Father Dale, speaking in code, "I see. Well sometimes at your age it is better to be quiet."

"Are you sure you haven't sinned in any other way?" Father asks prompting for her to give up all her misdeeds.

"I didn't tell the truth." Grace maintains.

"Let us hear your prayer of confession, " Father Dale instructs with a nod.

Having to participate in the sacrament of confession to this imposter weighs heavily against her better instincts. Grace is feeling a betrayal of her conscience while reluctantly making the sign of the cross.

Grace recites the prayer, "Bless me Father for I have sinned. This is my first confession. I lied."

Appealing to a higher celestial authority, she says, "My God, I am sorry for my sins with all my heart. In failing to do good, I have sinned against *You* whom I should love above all things. I firmly intend, with *Your help*, to sin no more, and to avoid whatever leads me to sin. Amen."

As she opens her eyes, Father Dale is examining her and then quickly breaks away to quickly recite, "God the Father of mercies, through the death and resurrection of his Son has reconciled the world to himself and sent the Holy Spirit among us for the forgiveness of sins; through the ministry of the Church may God give you pardon and peace, and I absolve you, Grace from your sins in the name of the Father, and of the Son and the Holy Spirit."

Grace leaves the office, looking to her classmates' faces as they await their first confession, ignorant of this man's duplicity.

~ 10 ~

MOTHER'S LITTLE HELPER

Grace has returned home from her day at school. Liliane is in the kitchen waiting for her.

Liliane tells her, "I asked Father Dale about your confession. How did it go?"

Grace, discouraged by her mother's intrusion of a private sacrament, "I told him I lied."

Liliane, "What did you lie about, Grace?"

Grace offers her mother a coded response while rolling her eyes, "As in, I didn't tell the truth."

Liliane taken aback by her sassiness, "That's not the same as lying, Grace."

Not wanting to face the local pharmacist, Liliane opens her wallet to pull out 4 white sheets of paper and bills of money to give to Grace. She says, "Grace, I need you to pick

78

up my prescription at the pharmacy. Here's the money and here are my prescriptions. You can buy yourself a chocolate bar with the change. Can you do that for Mummy?" Grace imagines a chocolate bar all to herself, a Twix bar or box of Smarties? "Okay. I will go on my bike."

Grace places the bills of money in her front pockets with the folded prescriptions. She grabs her 1980s style brown banana seat bike. A bike her father picked out for her, selecting his favourite color. This time she knows to take the long way to avoid the PQ'ist house where she was chased the day before. Along this longer route, the houses are larger and the front gardens are elaborate landscape displays.

Grace gives 4 prescription sheets over the counter with the bills of money her mother gave her. The Pharmacist is silent and looks at the young child. Taking the money and reviewing the prescriptions, he pushes one prescription back. In his voice, Grace can detect he holds a poor opinion of her mother, *"Ta mère doit visiter son médecin pour celui-là. Elle a pris trop."* Grace, lacking full context interprets 'elle a pris trop' as something bad. He returns to Grace the change. A ten-dollar bill and coins, confirming how long, *"Dix minutes."* Waiting for the prescriptions to be filled, Grace uses fifty cents to buy herself a box of Smarties. Sucking on the small candy coated chocolates, Grace scans an in store billboard *Maisons À Vendres*. The latest property listings for the adjacent real estate office with pictures and descriptions. She compares the prices of the most beautiful homes and which of these had an in ground pool or even a private tennis court. Moving on she looks through the make-up section, recognizing Shannon's favourite L'Oréal lip gloss.

"Madame Bailey." Her mother's name is called out from the other side of the Pharmacist counter. Conscious to convince the Pharmacist that her mother was a good, Grace smiles politely bidding him adieu, *"Merci Monsieur. Bonne journée."* Carefully wrapping the white paper bag around the grip of her right bike handle, Grace mounts her bike to journey home. Taking in all the beautiful houses and gardens, yearning for the kind of life she imagines only possible in these households. In her right hand, the white paper bag of her mother's prescription drugs swings forward and back as she pedals.

Arriving home she delivers the white bag to her mother. Acknowledging to her mother the unfilled prescription, relaying innocently the Pharmacist's message, "He said you have to see your doctor again for one of them."

Liliane feeling slightly exposed goes to the kitchen phone pulling the receiver off the wall, *"Ma fille viens de retourner avec mes medicaments. Pourquoi dois-je voir mon médecin? Pourquoi vous pouvez pas remplir mon ordonnance? J'ai besoin de ce médicament!"*

Grace listens carefully, unable to understand the exact meaning behind each word, she feels for the emotion in Liliane's reaction. Her mother replies defensively, *"Bin, au besoin...comme une ou deux fois par jour."*

Liliane incredulous, *"Une fois ou deux fois par semaine?"*

"Voyons don! Non Monsieur. S'il vous plaît non. Pas du tout. Elle n'est pas trop jeune pour faire des courses pour sa mère." Liliane hangs up the phone. Disagreeable following this exchange, she glances at Grace accusingly. Looking at her pill bottles, she pops one bottle open to take one little pill. Going to the sink to fill a glass a water. That she drinks.

"I'll just have my brandy." Shaking her head in irritated disbelief, she approaches the sideboard console in the dining room. Taking out a tulip-shaped glass, she pours herself a drink. Leaning up against the console she calms herself by swirling the liquid and inhaling the notes from the liquor.

Grace goes to her room to practice violin. She closes her bedroom door behind. Tightening her bow, and taking out her instrument to play Twinkle Twinkle Little Star. Her fingers positioning while running notes in her mind - *La La Mi Mi un un Mi, trois trois, deux deux, un un La. Mi mi trois trois deux deux La. La La Mi Mi...*

"GRACE!" Liliane yells, "NOT NOW! MY NERVES!" Grace with a dose of fear pounding in her heart puts her violin away back into its soft plush case. Carefully, loosening the horse hair's tension of her bow. Wishing she could shrink small enough to enter through the swirl of her violin's f-hole to hide inside where all the most beautiful symphonies were stored.

When enough time has passed and Liliane's second glass of Brandy has kicked in, Grace carefully walks on the path egg shells to the kitchen for a glass of milk. In a cheery voice Liliane asks her, "Grace, how would you like to go horseback riding?"

Grace replies excitedly, "Really?"

Liliane asks, "Guess who wants to take you?"

With happiness Grace exclaims, "Dad?" Oh, how wonderful, she's always wanted to go horseback riding.

Liliane says, "Father Dale! Dale said, he always wanted a daughter before becoming a priest..."

Grace appalled by the notion, "He's NOT MY FATHER. I HATE HIM and I Hate how you are with him! You don't get to rent me out as his make believe daughter like 'Meggie' in your dumb show! I hate him, his jokes, his smell! I hate how he is with Cana!"

Father Dale has made a practice of secretly approaching the family dog to discourage her from barking when he visits. Grace witnessing this inappropriate manipulation of Cana's natural role as the guardian of her family home. Sneaking her treats as though he was the horse whisperer of dogs.

Liliane explodes taking insult from Grace's defiant rejection. Hitting her daughter in a fit, while Grace covers her head for protection.

Yelling, "How dare you! How dare you! You have no idea how much he has done for me! YOU ARE NOT ALLOWED TO FEEL THAT WAY! You stay in your room. I don't want to see your face. I tried to do something nice for you! You ungrateful brat!"

Shannon has returned home, rushing in to pull her mother off of Grace. Shouting, "Mom! Stop! Stop! Stop! What are you doing?" Shannon is holding her mother's forearm tight and squeezing while looking at her in the eye. At fifteen she is taller, stronger from swim training and unintimidated to protect her little sister. She lets her mother go to hold Grace who is crying under her wing.

Liliane, grabbing her bag of prescriptions turns scornfully to address Grace while viciously pointing her finger, " Grace. You are never to speak to me like that again."

Avoiding any eye contact with Shannon, she picks up her glass of Brandy and retreats to her bedroom.

Shannon tries to comfort her little sister. Crouching down to meet Grace at eye level, she asks, "Grace, What did you say?" Grace unable to get her words out. Choking on her tears," "Fffff, Fffff, Father Dale. I don't want to go. He smells. I don't like him. I don't like him."

Shannon notices a red mark at the tail of Grace's eye. She kisses it better and says. "Grace, You don't have to go anywhere, you don't want to. I'll talk to Dad when he gets home."

Later, Shannon has a conversation with her father about what happened pointing to her mother's obsessive entanglement with Father Dale. "Dad, it's gone too far and people are noticing. I have classmates making fun of her need for his approval. Their parents are making fun of her."

Anxious at this revelation, he asks Shannon, "What are they saying?"

"Dad don't make me repeat. Why are you allowing her to spend so much time with him. He isn't helping things. Things are getting worse." Confronted by his daughter's reasoning, Frank has to face the reality of this intrusion.

Frank replies, "When the time is right, I'll speak with your mother later this evening."

Frank weighs confronting his confessor, Father Dale. Concluding the priest will only invert his dogmatic authority against him and wedge a wider division between he and Liliane.

Since her fit of rage, Liliane has repeatedly tried to phone, Father Dale. His counselling sessions reinforcing a one-sided belief that she could do no wrong, pushing her into a singular dependence on him, thus alienating her from the only family she had.

Later that evening Frank enters their bedroom. Knocking gently at the door he says, "Liliane, I'd like to talk about what happened with Grace."

At her bedside table is a half-filled tulip glass of brandy and a half-empty bottle. Liliane is holding the phone receiver to her ear, and the call is ringing on the other end. Unanswered from the other end, she hangs up the receiver.

"What did Shannon tell you?" Liliane asks angrily, interpreting Shannon's intervention as a betrayal of loyalty.

As calmly as he can manage Frank says, "Shannon said she had to pull you off of Grace."

Unrepentant, "Shannon wasn't here to hear how Grace spoke to me! You didn't hear what she said. Unbelievable, I just couldn't let her say such things!"

Frank pleading with her to see reason, "Liliane, what did Grace say?" His voice unconvinced anything Grace said, could have warranted the violent reaction Shannon described.

"You're saying I'm a bad mother!" Liliane trying to run away from the shadow her behavior has cast. She gets up to grab her purse. Rummaging to find her car keys. Frank insists, "No, Liliane. No. You do many wonderful things for our family but I am trying to talk reason to you about what happened today." Liliane pulls out her car keys from her purse.

Frank tells her, "Liliane you shouldn't be driving in this state!"

"I'm crazy now? I need to find Dale!" Liliane rushes out the door.

"Please Liliane, don't drive like this! It's dangerous!" Frank walks with her as she gets into the car. At the very least, he tries to get her to calm down before she drives off in a frenzy.

He returns inside. Checking in on Grace, Tommy and Shannon to wish them all good night. Deciding to take Cana for a late-night walk, he gets her on her leash and goes around the block. The stars are out and the night is peaceful. As he returns home, he sees headlights turn into his driveway. Relieved, he thinks there she's come back.   Only it's not their station wagon. It's a police car. He rushes back. Liliane is stepping out of the passenger seat, he runs to her side to help her. She's wearing a big round neck brace, he asks her "What happened?" The Officer tells him, *"Désolé M. Bailey, Ta femme elle a l'aire d'être maganée mais tout est correct. Malheureusement, ton char est complètement fini."* Liliane translates for Frank, "The car just spun out of control and another car hit me from behind while it was spinning. My neck is hurt but nothing came up on the X-ray and the other driver is fine. Thank God!"

The Officer approaches Frank to hand him the incident report, *"Pour votre réclamation d'assurance."* Frank stunned, looks over the report.

The officer nods, leans in slightly, suggests, *"Peut-être que vous devriez penser à prendre des cours... de conduite? Ça pourrait être utile, non?"* Liliane irritated translates for Frank, "He thinks we need conduct lessons!"

Humbled by the evening's events, Frank thanks the officer with his best french, *"Merci Monsieur l'agent. Je vous souhaite une bonne nuit."* Holding Liliane's arm in his, he helps her walk up the driveway to their front door. Reassuringly, he tells her, "I'll phone in work tomorrow to let them know I need to take the day off and Friday. That way I can help you around the house and arrange for a car rental."

Frank asks her again, "Liliane, are you okay? Did a doctor see you?"

"I'll be okay. I just hurt my neck," Liliane says. "The doctor gave me codeine for the pain." Worried by her behavior earlier she asks, "Is Grace okay? "

"She's sleeping." Frank answers. He assists Liliane to bed, setting pillows behind her comfortably so she can sleep with her neck brace.

Liliane drowsy, slurring her words, tells Frank, "Let Grace know she can come home tomorrow instead of going to her friend's house after school. She wanted so much to go to Carla's house. But since you'll be home maybe she rather come home after school, to be with you for an extra long weekend."

Frank turns out the light and closes the door behind him.

Unable to shake the anxiety from the events of the day, Frank finds himself pacing the living room holding his rosary, saying *Hail Marys*. To avoid waking Liliane or aggravating the injury to her neck, he opts to sleep on the living room couch.

Lying there overwhelmed by complex emotions, Frank's obsessive tendencies compel him to fixate on rooting out the evil he believes has infiltrated their home.

~ 11 ~

ROSEMARY'S BABY

It's Saturday morning and arguing can be heard between Shannon and Frank from outside the Bailey house. The neighbour from across the street, pauses tending his front garden to listen to the conflict.

Shannon shouting, "Dad! It's just a book, it's fiction."

Frank is in Shannon's bedroom and has discovered Shannon reading a copy of the novel, *Rosemary's Baby*. He insists, "Shannon, give it to me. Give me the book."

"Why?" Shannon asks him.

Frank tells her, "I want to see it. Let me read it with your mother." Shannon reluctantly hands him the book.

He leaves her room to examine the book from the living room. Moments pass and Frank has stepped out in the front yard and is holding a match to the book. Shannon watching from the window, runs to grab the extinguisher while shouting, "No Dad! It's a library book!"

Bursting through the front door, Shannon stands off opposite her father, holding an extinguisher. The wind has taken out the flame, "It's a library book. I have to return it." She points the extinguisher's hose at him, as he is trying to light another match.

Nodding his head, Frank insists, "You have been corrupted by the words of this book. The evil spirit in this book. We need a prayer circle. We need an exorcist."

Shannon pleads with him, looking around not wanting to draw more attention from their neighbours, more quietly she tries to speak reason. "Stop. This is so embarrassing. How am I going to explain?"

He replies, "I'll gladly go to your school and make sure there are never any copies of this book, AGAIN!"

Frank holds a lit match to the pages. Shannon sprays the extinguisher at her father, he turns his back to shield the flame from being extinguished. The whole book has caught flames, as he holds it from the corner of the hardcover. He is running away from her praying.

"Our Father, who art in Heaven, Hallowed be thy name. Thy Kingdom Come, thy will be done....Hail Mary Full of Grace..."

The neighbours across the street laugh to each other as the drama unfolds before them.

"Tabarnak sont fous. Les osti religieux!" First neighbour says to the other, a woman.

"Bon, j'ai appelé les pompiers. Sont des fanatiques irlandais catholiques. Par contre, la femme, elle est québécoise. Une orpheline élevée par les soeurs grises."

"Ah ouais? La folle?"

The book's pages are half charred. Shannon says, "It's not your property. You will have to pay the fine."

Frank sternly tells her, "Shannon, you will pay the fine as your punishment for having taken this book out in the first place. Bringing this kind of book into our home, reading as much filth and devil worship."

Sirens can be heard in the background. Liliane comes out, "Frank? The fire department is coming..."

He replies looking over to Liliane, confident he's rooted out the evil that has infiltrated his family home, "Well these are the fires of hell. Let them come extinguish them as we pray." Liliane steps out to join Frank and pray as the last pages of *Rose Mary's Baby* burns.

Across, the street the neighbour translates what he's overheard, *"Les feux de l'enfer sont dans le livre!"* They shake their heads as the absurdity unfolds with Frank and Liliane praying out loud in English.

Shannon throws down the extinguisher and grabs her bike, "So embarrassing. You're both *fucking* crazy!" Just as the fire truck pulls in, Shannon bikes out of their driveway. A young handsome firemen smiles at her awkwardly pedal her bike, in tears and humiliated.

Liliane to Frank, "The profanity! She's possessed?"

Translating to the neighbour, *"Possédée par des démons?!"* She replies while laughing sympathetically, *"Ah, quelle honte. Pauvre fille."*

Neighbour yells out to them, *"Eh, eh? Liliane? Ici au Québec, Dieu parle que le Francais! Liliane, il faut prier en Français!"*

Liliane scoffs, before translating to Frank, "Tsk, he's telling us to pray in French! He says God's French!"

Shannon bikes to her best friend Nat's house. Knocking at the door, Shannon is surprised when Sebastian answers. He is home for a visit from University, "Hi! Come in. Nat will be back in an hour or two. You look upset."

Shannon enters the home. "My parents, they are so fucking nuts. My dad's crazy!"

He asks, "What happened?"

"He burnt my book!"

Sebastian laughs, "What?"

Shannon elaborates, "On the front lawn. The neighbours were watching. You'd think they would send someone to take them away to a Mental Hospital!"

Sebastian, curious about the development, "What book?"

Shannon, sighs at the thought, "A library book. *Rosemary's Baby*. Now I have to tell the librarian my father burnt the copy I took out."

Sebastian tells her, "No you don't." He runs upstairs. Peeking his head back from the top, "Come, I've got something for you."

Shannon follows Sebastian up to his bedroom. He opens his closet moving through a pile of books on the top shelf. "Here it is!" Then grabs a second book and says, "Ah! And this one!" Comes out with two books.

"Here. You can return this copy." He hands her his copy of *Rosemary's Baby.* Pleased at being able to solve her problem. "Hardcover right? And here's another one that will drive your parents to insanity."

Sebastian holds up a copy of *The Exorcist.* "Scary stuff. I've read them. And actually, now that I know they're a fire hazard..." She laughs, taking the book.

Shannon hasn't seen Sebastian up close for a couple of years since he went away to school. His swim meet medals hang on a hook inside his closet. He's grown out and up in a pleasant and attractive way that brings a smile to her face just being in his presence.

"I don't know what to say. This is the exact book cover and version I borrowed. It's just missing the library insert and school stamp. Thank you, Sebastian. I'll have to hide this one, though." Shannon taps his copy of *The Exorcist.*

"He said he's going to the school and demand a book banning."

Sebastian takes *Rosemary's Baby* from her hands. Opens it, going through the pages he asks, "What page were you at?"

"Around one-eighty, before my father barged in this morning!" Sebastian jumps on his bed and invites Shannon to sit beside him. Patting his bed cover he says, "Let's read it, together." She hesitates, he gestures his open hand like a Bob Barker beauty, "If you prefer the chair."

Shannon looks at the chair and decides to sit beside Sebastian on his bed. There's a familiarity from the years of being close with Nat and having trained with him at the same swim club.

"There's only sixty-five pages left. Since I am giving you my copy, to rescue you from the embarrassment of explaining what Saint Francis did, you read and I'll listen."

Shannon agrees, " Fair enough. I'll read to you."

Just as she sits up to begin reading, Sebastian pulls the book down to say laughing, "Rosemary really knows how to pick a Guy, eh?"

Shannon smiles replying, "And an apartment, she should have listened to Hutch!"

"*M. Bailey, Pas une bonne idée de brûler des livres sur votre pelouse.*" In thick québécois accent, he repeats, "Not a good idea to burn things in an uncontrolled manner. A spark could have caught and spread, putting your house and the house of your neighbour's on fire."

Frank repentant, "I understand. I am afraid I didn't think of that."

The Fire Chief asks, "What was the book?"

Frank answers, "I rather not say. It's behind us now."

"M. Bailey, burn things in your backyard BBQ or your fireplace if you have one. Also, there was a complaint about the yelling and intense chanting?"

Not wanting to be a 'Peter', "I was praying to our Lord."

Addressing Liliane, "*S'il vous plaît, Monsieur et Madame Bailey, respectez le droit de vos voisins à profiter tranquillement de leurs week-ends.*"

The line between routing out evil and extending the courtesy of tranquility to one's neighbour had previously not factored into Frank's consideration.

The Firemen do a final scan to ensure no cinders may reignite. *Les voisins,* unimpressed return back inside their homes as the Fire Truck drives away.

Liliane tells Frank, "Let Shannon stay at her friends today. We'll watch out for her behaviour, knowing she's read that book. I'll ask Dale for signs to look for...you know?" Whispering to Frank, "For demonic footholds?" She tries to nod but her face is pushed upward by the foam braced wrapped around her neck. Her awkward stiffness exposing

Liliane's disembodied logic and the demonic forces at the root of her mental state.

Shannon turns the page, "Fifteen more pages."

Sebastian turns on his side to watch Shannon as she reads. She stops reading to look at him watch her. She says, "What?" Sebastian asks, "How old are you?"

Shannon answers with a smile, "Same age as Nat." He smiles back, "Right." He pauses and asks, "Do you have a boyfriend?" Shannon blushing avoids a direct answer, "Don't distract me. Let me finish reading."

At the Bailey home, Liliane wearing her neck brace is making an emergency phone call to Father Dale. She has no choice but to leave a voice message with his call service. "It's urgent. I need him to phone me back, right away. It can't wait for tomorrow. The devil has come into our home and Father Dale's the only one we can turn to. Please have him call me back."

Frank now doubtful comes in, " Maybe, I overreacted. All the yelling, disturbing the neighbours. And now Shannon is God knows where?"

Liliane urges him, "You can't go back on what you said, Frank. You have to stay firm. You apologize now and she'll question your judgement about everything."

Frank says, "She already does, Liliane. That Chalice we bought, did the Church really need another Chalice?"   Liliane astounded, "My Chalice? You're bringing that up now? Surely, the Devil has come into our home with that book. See how it's sowed division between us?"

Frank challenges her, "You're blaming the book?"

Sebastian leans in and pulls the book down. Tells Shannon, "You don't have to read anymore." He kisses Shannon softly on her cheek, pulling away to see her expression and back closer again to gently kiss her lips.

Shannon happily stunned, "What if I had a boyfriend?"

Sebastian asks, "You don't?"

"No." They are interrupted by noises and voices at the front door. Nat has returned with her parents from grocery shopping.

Sebastian touches his finger to his lips, saying, "I can keep it secret, if you can."

Together they head downstairs. Shannon holding the two books. "Hi Nat! Your brother let me in to wait for you."

Nat replies, "Cool, I was just about to call you. What's up?" Sebastian heads to the kitchen to help with the groceries. Shannon calling after him, "Thanks again Seb, for the books."

The girls run back upstairs to Nat's bedroom. Nat closes her door behind them. Shannon says, "Your brother is so sweet."

Nat excited the way girls get, "Do you have a crush on him?"

"I came here crying and upset, because my parents are mental. My dad burnt my library version of *Rosemary's Baby*. And he gave me his copy. And a copy of *The Exorcist!*" Shannon holds up the books.

Nat says, "Not exactly romantic tales." Nat jumps onto her bed and continues, "Shannon, I don't understand your parents. Your Dad is so intense about everything Catholic and then ignores what is right in front of him. Like Tommy. He's such a bully. He's funny, but vicious cruel. He got everyone laughing at Tammy and she's three grades older than him. Ridiculing the effort she puts into her hair, and clothes. She just sat there, stunned and exposed!"

Shannon curious, "Did she cry?"

Nat tells her, "No but...he got in her head, imitating her picking out her clothes and her deciding how to set a side ponytail in front of her mirror. *EVERYONE* was laughing at her and she had to sit there and take it. She eventually laughed too."

Shannon, sighs, "Sebastian is the complete opposite. You're so lucky." Nat agrees, "Yah. I love my brother. He leaves tomorrow to head back to school. Do you want to sleep over?"

Shannon torn, it will be months before she'll get to see him again, "I have to babysit."

Nat excited, "Come over after you finish. We'll watch a movie!"

Later at home, Frank is looking for Tommy and goes into his bedroom which is a mess. Liliane passes by the doorway. She looks in, with her head propped up in her neck brace, "What a pig sty! Frank, I wish you would get him to clean his room. And look over there," Liliane points to a desk that a canvas is set on with jars of solvent, brushes, plastic trays full of blotches of paints. "He's going to get paint on his clothes and the bed sheets."

Frank thinking out loud, "Maybe we can set up an art studio in the basement?"

Liliane, "Wow! If you could noise proof it, that would be great!"

He replies, "One thing at a time Liliane. I'll drive Grace to her violin lessons."

The phone rings in the background. Liliane rushes to take the call privately from her bedroom.

Liliane answers, "Hello? ... Dale, just a minute." She closes her bedroom door behind her. Frank sneaks up to the door to eavesdrop on her conversation. Hearing her description highlighted the absurdity. Finding he can't bear to listen to her go over the events of the morning and emphatically conclude that Shannon must be possessed.

Another ploy inviting Father Dale's intervention for a make-believe crisis.

~ 12 ~

VIOLIN LESSONS

Grace has shown up behind Frank with her violin. She says, "Ready, Papa!"

Frank replies, " Right. Violin lessons. Have you been practicing?"

Grace tells him, "When I can. Mum tells me to stop because of her nerves. The noise is too much." Frank disappointed, "You need to practice if you are to be any good."

Grace feeling guilty admits, "I know."

Just as they are leaving the house, Tommy gets in Grace's path and makes a gesture of himself playing the violin badly, squishing his face and sounding a terribly unpleasant screech.   Waiting for his father to move beyond ear range, he taunts her in a cunning and matter of fact tone, "Grace, if only you were born with natural talent, Mum could bear to listen."

On the drive to her lesson, Grace quietly looks out the window. A question that hadn't occurred to her before pops in her mind, "Papa, how did you meet Mum?"

Frank answers, "Bishop Cavanagh introduced us at a St. Patrick's Church meeting. He was Father Cavanagh at the time."

"When you were younger, did you know women who didn't go to Church?" As many parents do, Frank makes a calculation, first on age appropriateness of his reply and second the consequences of an opening for more questions he ought not answer.

Franks decides that providing an educational and informative response, "Yes. There are women at my work who don't go to Church. Some people follow a different religion and so they go to Temple or Synagogue. Muslim women will go to a Mosque." While he risked introducing Grace to the concept of other religions, this was the most effective reply to avoid disclosing the actual mature truth of the *kinds of women* he knew when he was younger, inasmuch he assumed *certainly did not* attend Church.

At her music lesson, Grace sets up her music book and when given the go-ahead by her Instructor, she begins to play *Frère Jacques*. A melody she was given as homework to practice. Grace's instructor asks how many hours she practiced playing her violin in the last week. Grace tears up and says her Mum asked her to stop playing.

The remainder of her lesson, her Instructor has her play scales and replay the song. Guiding the positioning of her fingers and how she holds the instrument and her bow.

At the end of the lesson, the Instructor speaks to Frank privately. In a French accent, he tells him, *"She needs to practice at least, dee absolute minimum tree hours a week. It's dee most difficult instrument to master."*

The next month of lessons is fifty dollars. Frank takes his wallet out, pulls out a few bills. Reluctant to part with his money, keeps shuffling the bills between his thumb and index finger. Grace interprets this as a sign her father doesn't believe in the value of her talent and desire to play violin.

The drive home, Grace in the back seat begins to sob to herself. At first a little and then uncontrollably, holding her violin. Her father tries to talk reason, "Grace, you heard your instructor. You have to practice more."

"Mom doesn't want me to. And she doesn't want me home so she can be with Father Dale!"

Frank alarmed, "Why doesn't she want you home? Why do you say that?"

Grace replies, "She told me I can't tell. Because, people will be jealous."

"I don't understand. What people would be jealous?" Frank is questioning, does she mean 'People' as in him. He thinks *No. Grace is mixed up about her mother's strange expectations around Father Dale.*

"Speak of the devil," Frank says as he spots Father Dale's car parked at a home of a fellow Parishioner. There he is, Mr. Charismatic in the driveway hugging a woman closely. But wait, if his rear-view mirror hasn't deceived him, he sees the priest kissing her hand!

The remainder of the drive home, Grace continues to sniffle in the backseat. Frank finds himself ruminating how Father Dale spiritually extorted him into waiting until Liliane has gone through Menopause to have intimate relations *with his own wife!*

All so the fox could get in his hen house.

~ 13 ~

NINE TO FIVE

After a hectic weekend and another Sunday where despite her injury, Liliane must have lunch with Father Dale. This time wearing her neck brace. Frank returns to work questioning the relationship between his mood and Father Dale's undue influence over his wife. Could it be that his obsessive pride of fully devoting himself to Catholic Doctrine has painted him into a corner controlled by the Devil?

Pouring himself a coffee in the staff kitchen. "That bugger is clever!" He utters to himself. A colleague walking in to place his prepared lunch in the fridge asks, "What bugger?"

Frank says half joking, "Satan. The devil's in the details you know?"

His colleague, a german architect named Hans, agrees by adding, "God is in the detail but the Devil, *he is in the details.* Like legal contracts, fine print. All those areas we don't want to look, because we are prone to self-deception."

"Self-deception?" Frank asks intrigued. Realizing just at this moment what is the point of honesty, if there is a part of ourselves that refuses to face the truth?

Hans out loud, quite passionately says, "Wanting to believe something is true, when it's *false*. Our psyche is lurking in the shadow, running the show," he points to his mind. "It happens all the time, even here with intelligent teams."

"Hans, I need a fresh perspective. Someone outside my circle. Objective private feedback. Psychoanalysis of my own self-deception."

"Dr. Rhona Rosenthal. Look her up." Hans says. "She lectures at the university and her office is on Greene Avenue."

"Rosenthal?" Frank asks to confirm. Hans nods, pouring himself a coffee.

Frank returns to his desk. Quickly pulls out the phone book, to write down the address and telephone number for a Dr. Rhona Rosenthal on a note pad. Looking through the yellow pages he finds her listing. *Dr. Rhona Rosenthal, Jungian Psychotherapist.* He tears off the sheet, folds it and slips the small note of paper into his wallet.

Taking a sip of his coffee, he picks up a mechanical pencil, turning to his engineering blueprints for the latest project.

~ 14 ~

BOYS WILL BE BOYS

It's evening and the final episode is airing of *ABC's Made for TV* version of *The Thorn Birds*. Liliane with her two eldest children are watching Father de Briccasssart crying, reaching out to Meggie having just learned that it was in fact his biological son, Dane whom he just buried.

Liliane is sobbing uncontrollably. Shannon watching her mother, glances over to her brother rolling her eyes, then looks back to the TV. Liliane blows her nose, sobs, Tommy shakes his head and smirks devilishly at Shannon before saying, "Weird scene when Dane was undressing Father Dale. I mean Father Dale. I mean Father *RALPH!*" He concludes," Pretty lame."

Shannon and Tommy start laughing. Liliane angered by both of them says, "Tommy you have to ruin everything!"

Shannon, laughing through her words, "I guess Dane slept at Cardinal Ralph's place all those years, a special arrangement. Just like Meggie."

Liliane gets up angry and grabs her tulip glass, trying to ignore her teenagers' remarks. She then turns accusingly pointing to them and then to the television, "You both think you're funny. You want to ruin a nice movie with stupid jokes!"

Frank is at the desk in the study going over bills and letters, writing cheques for bill payments. Liliane comes to speak with him. " Frank, I think we should rewrite our wills. I would like Father Dale to be the executor to look after the children if anything were to happen to us."

Bewildered he answers, "We just updated our wills last summer. My sister will be insulted if she learns we've changed it."

Liliane trying to convince him, "She lives so far away and we aren't close, like we are with Father Dale. I have already spoken about it with him and he has agreed." She pats him on his shoulder and adds, "Frank, Dale has been so very good to you."

Frank sighs, "I wish you came to me first before getting him to volunteer for another role that involves our family?"

"You know how your sister treated me. The things she said to me about my past and how lucky someone like me with my background could be to marry you! And the way she treated me when I went to visit her ranch. She had me sleep on a thin mattress on the floor. I have the paperwork all done by the Notary, it's just a name change requiring your signature."

Frank works to maintain his composure, "Liliane, my sister is Grace's godmother. Whose idea was this?"

Liliane tells him,"Mine. I don't like your sister. She thinks she's better than me! She'll say horrible things about me."

Frank continues, "As it is now, there aren't significant assets if something were to happen to both of us, or me. Just the Insurance with the Order of Engineers and the Mortgage Insurance. The interest rates on the credit cards and how the Sears Card are all racked up and you want a new couch, what's the colour? Pink?"

Liliane protests raising her voice, "It's *Ashes of Roses*! We need a new living room set. I need this colour to lift my mood. The other couch, you chose is so depressing and dreary." Frank is beginning to see how the pattern in Liliane's impulse spending is driven by her mood.

"Liliane, I can't agree to this. I have to talk with *Dale* to discuss my concerns. At a minimum, let me read the paperwork and sleep on it. If we are changing it, I want to make sure it's reflective of the kids' needs and their age. Shannon will be an adult in less than three years.

Liliane angered, "You don't think I can handle a will? I'm not smart enough?"

The disagreement can be heard from the washroom as their teenagers take turns brushing their teeth. Shannon perplexed, "What are they arguing about?"

"Let's put it this way Shannon, Mrs. Mary Carson wants to leave Drogheda to Cardinal Ralph and the Roman Catholic Church instead of her sister-in-law." Tommy draws a parallel to *The Thorn Birds* narrative. His mother's obsession with the priest, her new favourite color, *Ashes of Roses*, and now her fixation on leaving their estate to Father Dale, all so comically and painfully absurd.

Shannon dumbfounded by her mother's behavior, "I could have died! Rob Leblanc brought Mom up at Val's party and how she's always chasing after Father Dale. Then he called Dad a cuckold."

Tommy shrugs to say, "I don't know what that is." Spits his toothpaste into sink, rinses and places his toothbrush. Wiping a towel to his face before exiting the washroom.

Shannon continues to wash her face and brush her hair. Laughing again at how she and Tommy joked about the final emotionally intense scene between *Meggie and Father Ralph de Briccassart.* Their sense of humour being the most sane response to their mother's entanglement.

The next day, Liliane is visibly disturbed having received a phonecall about Tommy. Yelling to her husband, "FRANK! FRANK! I just got off the phone with Cindy McIntyre. What's a circle jerk?"

Frank walking upstairs from the basement, "A what?"

Liliane tells him, "Tommy! He's been caught with his friends in an underground fort they built with stolen wood. The Police just found them with pornographic magazines in a circle jerk! What is that?" Frank is stunned.

"You have to go get him. The Police are there with Angus, James, Dirk and JP and I don't know who else but this is horrible! Disgusting!"

Franks asks again, "In the woods?"

Drawn to the intensity, Grace is in the hallway listening to the commotion.

Liliane says, "Yes! They made an underground cave or something and covered it with dirt over stolen wood from a home construction site. The owner is pressing charges. Wait til Dale hears about this!"

Frank beaten down by her mention of that name. He says, "I'll go find him and speak to the Police."

He leaves the house from the back door and not so far behind, Grace follows her father hiding behind trees.

When Frank arrives to the Fort in the woods, Tommy and his friends are standing holding their groin without any clothes on. Waiting as each of their fathers arrive to negotiate the impending charges for larceny and mischief with the Police.

Grace hiding behind a tree in the forest, watches on to witness her older bully brother naked and humiliated, crying. Three Police Officers are present speaking to the other two fathers of Tommy's friends. One Police Officer walks over to greet her father, Frank.

The Officer speaks a fluent English, "Mr. Bailey, your son with his friends were seen by the owner stealing this wood from a home construction site. Unless you can convince the owner of the stolen property otherwise, we will be referring your son for juvenile prosecution along with the other boys for theft."

Angus McIntyre, James and Dirk's father is livid. He's a big burly man with a big horseshoe style moustache. "I caught them in my basement doing the same thing, watching one of my movies, James took. I told them to go do it in the woods. They stole half my magazines!" Angus shakes a rolled up magazine above his head and hits the back side of his two sons' heads.

Frank unimpressed, "As a father and husband, maybe you shouldn't have those filthy magazines? You have a daughter!"

Angus replies shouting, "Oh! All pious, Saint Francis and his joker son!"

Frank catches a smirk from one of the Officers. A second wave of embarrassment washes over as he recognizes the Officer that drove Liliane home after her car accident. He's observing Frank, pressing his lips together with a knowing crinkle in his eye. Appealing to the English speaking Officer, throwing his arms up Frank pleads, "Can't they put their clothes back on?"

The Officer gives the okay and the boys rush to cover themselves. Hopping to grab their briefs and get their feet into their pants legs as fast as they can. The group of four boys with their fathers and the Police leave the sight.

After they have walked far enough away, Grace goes to the fort to see what it was. When underground, Grace sees the ripped pages of pornographic pictures pinned up on the dirt walls of the fort, and magazines left open on the ground. It is the first time she is exposed to this content.

Pictures of shinny women and men naked with erect penises in the dirt of this fort.

Back at their home, Liliane is at the kitchen table looking through a catalogue and on the phone with a sales agent. "Can I get it in *'Ashes of Roses'* How do you call it? *Vieux Rose*? Yes, I love that colour." Liliane writes down the price. Frank enters the back door with Tommy behind him.

She sees them enter and into the receiver says, "I'm sorry. I'll call back at a better time. Thank you!" Hanging up the phone she looks at her thirteen-year-old son. Tommy is unable to look her in the eyes.

"You're going to confession. Father Dale will have a good speaking to you to set you straight. I can't tell what is worse, stealing or what you boys were doing? They are both horrible. You should be ashamed of yourself. Caught with your pants down like that!"

Frank tells her, "Liliane, they have been sufficiently reprimanded and humiliated by the Police with consequence. I need to speak with the man they stole from. Let me take care of it."

She suggests, "What if Father Dale spoke to him?"

"NO! For once NO!" Frank answers flabbergasted.

"And what about his confession? What? Get him to write lines as punishment? What is he supposed to write? I don't want to read that. Disgusting and those MacIntyre boys, pigs like their father, Angus. He's the one who bought those magazines. They're perverts. Disgusting! Horrible!" Liliane goes on turning to Tommy. "Well what do you have to say for yourself?"

Grace returns home tentatively walking to the back door. From where their voices carry. Her absence has gone unnoticed, eclipsed by the drama and embarrassment Liliane and Frank feel. Entering the kitchen, Grace attempts an innocent return to the mundane. "Is dinner almost ready?"

Liliane turns to answer, "Almost. Good Lord Grace! Look at your knees! They are filthy! Go wash up, then come set the table." She shakes her head oblivious to the spill over into her daughter's mind.

"Tommy, go to your room and you will eat supper alone tonight. Think about what you've done." Tommy walks slowly with his head down to his bedroom."

Frank searching for solutions, concludes, "He has to go to private school."

Liliane agrees, "Right away. Loyola. They're bad stock those McIntyre brothers. Take after their father. Problem is,

Tommy misbehaves in class and that reputation will follow him."

Frank continues intensely, "The only hope is for him to be in a good school and surround him with a solid Catholic education to counter all this filth."

Shannon enters the kitchen to pour herself a glass of water. "I wanted to go to private school, you said it was too expensive. He'll never get accepted without a recommendation from his teachers. He's always humiliating them and making them the brunt of his jokes. ALL of them, except his art teacher."

Frank upset, "His art teacher is homosexual. I will find him a female art mentor."

Liliane confused, "Father Dale is his art mentor!"

Shannon intervenes with the voice of reason, "Mom! He needs a proper *art mentor* with an actual background in fine art. Father Dale is not an expert. Can't you see that?"

Liliane insulted,"You think I'm stupid? Shannon, he knows so many things. He's an expert in so many, in so many, what's the word....?" Liliane distracted whispers to Frank, "Frank? Frank? In a circle jerk, do they do it to each other or themselves?"

Frank now angered, "I don't know!"

Shannon continues, "Is he though? Have you actually seen him do all these things he claims to be an expert at? He's a phoney! And he's used religion to intrude into almost every aspect of our life. Now, now you want him to be the Executor of your's and Dad's will? Fuck! Mom, WAKE UP!"

Liliane, stunned by her daughter's challenge, "You have a problem with that Shannon? I have a good mind to write you out of our Will."

"What?" Shannon is taken aback.

Frank implores his wife, "Liliane?"

"You don't OWN anything, the house is mortgaged to the limit and all the extra money goes into the Church, including a ridiculous Chalice! And that ridiculous donation you made to Father Dale's *fund*."

Liliane defends their generosity, "For a children's school in Ethiopia!"

Shannon, feeling it better to be disowned by her mother than betray her conscience, "You verified that? What's the name of the school?"

Liliane, "Oh that's ridiculous. Where is all this coming from? What kind of books are making you think this way about a good man?"

Frank recalls a planned event, where donors were recognized for the scale of their generosity, depicted by the size of their brick in an illustrated school building. As Frank was filling out their donation cheque, Father Dale suggested, "Frank, for now leave the '*Pay to the Order*' blank. Vicki will fill it in for you when we confirm the exact spelling of the school fund. They are still deciding what Saint they want to commemorate for the building. Do you have a favourite Saint?"

Frank giving some consideration, "Saint Francis of Assisi. St. Micheal's, after the Arch Angel Michael."

"Frank, I'll recommend both of these." Father Dale writes down the Saint names on a small sheet of paper attaching with a paper clip to the cheque, smiling. "Your generosity is appreciated and will provide so much for these children."

Frank says, "I think Shannon has a point. Maybe we should broaden who we seek counsel from. It's too much for Father Dale to be the executor of our Will. My sister is already the legal executor. Better to keep these matters in the family. And maybe we need to open our minds to other solutions? Shannon will be eighteen in three years..."

Liliane interrupts him," I don't trust your sister."

Frank responds asking, "Liliane, Who do you trust?"

Liliane answers, "Dale. He's the only one telling me the truth."

Shannon and Frank look at each other. Their thoughts telepathic *Has she lost her mind?*

~ 15 ~

THE SHADOW

It's Monday. Frank is taking his lunch break to walk to Dr. Rhona Rosenthal's office is at Westmount Square. A meeting he was able to arrange on account of a last minute cancellation by one of her regular patients. In a building designed by a famous German architect, Mies van der Rohe and built fifteen years prior, that coincidentally Frank as an engineer had designed the electric system.

Something *grounding* in that, especially for an electric engineer. He was testing a humorous pun for Dr. Rhona. Her office was modern and simplistic. Walnut wood chairs with cushioned black leather, black and white photography for artwork hung on the walls. Straight to the point design.

Dr. Rosenthal was a mature woman, with extra large rim glasses. Her hair was all white, chin length with a gentle curl from being tucked behind her ear. Inviting Frank to sit, she sat across from him and asked," What brings you here, Mr. Bailey? Or do you prefer Frank?"

"Frank is fine. My wife Liliane, she has developed a dependence, a relationship with our Parish Priest." He manages to lean forward and lean back over and over while trying to express this one sentence.

"Has it become sexual?" She asked so casually, he didn't know what to say.

"What?" Dumbfounded, he must have heard wrong.

"Frank, what kind of relationship does your wife have with your priest?"

"Everything is Father Dale." Frank found himself squirming beneath her direct gaze. Questions are powerful, even when you don't answer or you evade them, once they are put out there, they linger until there is an answer.

"How do you think he maintains this level of influence over your wife?" She watches Frank as he considers this question.

"Uh, I don't know. It started after we saw him for marriage counselling." Franks too embarrassed to mention how the role had since expanded into Sunday lunches, Prayer meetings, Art mentoring and most recently if Liliane gets her way, inheriting his estate and the guardianship of his children.

"How did Father Dale help your marriage?" Did she only ask five questions that Frank had been too blind to ask himself? Regretful he answers, "Our marriage got worse after seeking his guidance."

She leans back letting that sink in. Maintaining eye contact, her pause is timed to perfection before she asks with sincere curiosity, "Frank, what kind of relationship would you like to have with Liliane?"

No one ever asked Frank such a question. He never asked himself. His focus was always a matter of what he or Liliane had to do or be, in order to make up for their sins of the past. Dr. Rosenthal's simple questions were like a magnifying lens over a faulty blueprint exposing the misguided priorities that had been governing his life.

Conceding defeat Frank admits, "I built my home on sand without realizing it."

Dr. Rosenthal ended with one final question, "Frank, how long has it been since you were sexually intimate with your wife?"

Afraid how silly he would sound, elaborating to a Jewish woman the details of his assigned penance by Father Dale, that he wait until his wife's menopause before having sex with her again. Embarrassed by how harshly he insisted Liliane be ready to carry and love more children.

Instead Frank confirmed, "Not since we started marriage counselling."

~ 16 ~

COURSE CORRECTION

Grace is drawing in her bedroom. She is working on a draft sketch of her house, where she has added a third floor level to expand the space. Pleased with her ingenuity she brings the drawing to her father.

He is in the living room, watching an interview on TV of the premier of Québec, René Lévesque discussing the impact of *Loi 2* and the importance of Sovereignty and self-determination of a people. The interview continues in the background, touching on the Silent Revolution and the breakaway from the Roman Catholic Church.

Looking briefly at the man smoking a cigarette on the television Grace asks, "Papa, can I show you my drawings?" Her father replies holding out his hand, "Show me, Grace." Grace climbs up onto Frank's lap. He holds her lovingly, kissing the top of her head.

"See, it's our house with an upstairs. I added a skylight and an open balcony. And here, I added walls to the carport to make it a garage. For the winter." Her drawing captures different perspectives of the new roof and the newly added space.

"What's this?" He points to a skylight. "That's my new bedroom, with another skylight to look at the stars."

"This is architecture," Frank tells her.

Grace excited replies, "Yah! That's what I want to be."

Frank suggests, "You can marry an architect."

Grace unamused, answers, "I don't want to marry an architect, I want to *be an architect*."

Tommy overhearing their exchange from the kitchen chimes in, " That's ok Grace, cause NO ONE will marry you."

Frank sobered by the recent consequences of his son's nature frowns to question him, "Tommy, is that a way to speak to your sister?"

Tommy unapologetic looks at Grace to say, "What doesn't kill her, will make her stronger." Not a moment too soon, Shannon walks through the living room. "So your bullying is to make her stronger?" The hierarchy of sibling rivalry playing out as Grace's eyes dart between her siblings and back to her father to measure her significance.

Tommy to Shannon claims, "Yes. It's for her own benefit. Grace will thank me later."

Grace contemplates Tommy's claim. Could his unrelenting dominance be the reason why she doesn't feel vulnerable to bullies at school? Or is her brother the only bully?

Tommy approaches Grace, "Let me see?"

The phone rings from the kitchen. As soon as Frank has left to answer the phone, Tommy grabs Grace's drawings. In the background Frank speaks into the receiver, "Hello?"

Grace is pleading and jumping to retrieve her drawings, "Give them back, Tommy. I don't want..." Tommy is laughing, keeping her drawings out of her reach and taunting her to make her cry.

Shannon intervenes, with a hint of righteous malice in her voice, "Let go, *STROKER*. She's seven. Grow up!"

Tommy, humiliated by Shannon's slur, throws Grace's drawings up in the air. Grace has to pick them up off the ground and flatten out the wrinkles he's caused by grasping the sheets of paper too tightly with his sweaty palms.

On the phone is an admissions advisor from Loyola Private High School for Boys. He informs Frank that Tommy is not a candidate for admission with a probationary juvenile charge for larceny, indecency, and mischief. Frank must accept that he is unable to get Tommy into a Catholic private school.

Inspired by Grace's drawings, Frank decides, he and Tommy will renovate a basement corner into an art studio where Tommy will remain occupied painting and out of Liliane's way.

Grace watches the last bit of René Lévesque speaking in French. A clip of Charles de Gaulle on a balcony to a crowd, *"Vive le Québec, Vive le Québec libre, Vive le Canada Français et Vive la Nouvelle France, Vive la France!"* Grace starts swinging her head humming along to the crowd of *Québecois* singing *La Marseillaise*. Like an antenna in her DNA, the anthem's trumpets awaken a thread to her lineage. *Allons les enfants de la Patrie, Le jour de Gloire est arrivé!*

Frank walks in to see her spirited marching, *Marchons, Marchons!* Grace recognizing the name of the figure proudly says to her father, "That man's name is the same as the street we drive on, *Boulevard de Gaulle!*"

Frank nods yes, "Let me see your drawings again?" He looks at the layout, "Where are the stairs?" She looks at him as though obvious, "Above the other stairs!" He gives her back her drawings.   Over hearing *La Marseillaise* a call to arms, Liliane has begun to sing from the other room. Frank turns off the television to hear her voice and the unofficial anthem of Québec:

Le temps que l'on prend pour dire Je t'aime

C'est le seul qui reste au bout de nos jours

Les voeux que l'on fait, les fleurs que l'on sème

Chacun les récolte en soi-même

Au beau jardin du temps qui court

She comes into the living room. Dancing with Frank for but a brief moment, as she sings:

Gens du pays, c'est votre tour

De vous laisser parler d'amour

Gens du pays, c'est votre tour

De vous laisser parler d'amour

A love song she would sing, adapting the lyrics for any of their birthdays when bringing out a lit up cake she had baked. Replacing Gens du pays with any of their names.

Just as though it was yesterday when he was first enchanted by her singing, Frank reminisces a time they lived together as newlyweds in Ireland.   At the town pub, everyone had to take their turn with a tune. When it came to Liliane, she chose to sing a Québec folksong *'Allouette, Gentile Allouette'*. She had the whole pub singing into the palm of her hand:

Et le bec (Liliane first),
et le bec (the pub back to her)
Et la tête (her),
et la tête (the pub) ...
Allouette (her)
Allouette (and the pub)
Oh oh oh oh! (Altogether cheering)

And so on back when they were fun, in love with each other and their future. Most importantly, governed by a mutual desire for closeness.

Frank tells Grace, "I'll ask an architect friend of mine at my work, Hans. But today, Tommy and I are going to start in the basement." Grace excited, runs after Shannon to share as Shannon prepares to leave for her new job, sorting books at the Library.

"Shannon, do you like my design? Dad's going to ask an architect at work. If we had a bigger house, then I won't have to leave on Thursdays." Grace is so pleased with the prospect.

Shannon asks her, "What??? Why do you have to leave on Thursdays?"

Grace confused if she was betraying her mother's instructions, hesitates to confirm, "Um, After school, when Father Dale visits." Shannon, unaware of this arrangement given that Tuesdays and Thursdays are when she has swim team practice. Shannon dismayed asks Grace again, "He comes on Thursdays?"

"Not the Thursday after her accident. But she said I can't be here when he visits. And mom told me not to tell anyone because they'll be jealous. I don't think she meant you, just that I couldn't tell anyone at school." Grace has that unpleasant feeling in her gut of misaligned loyalties. Did she just make a mistake that would lead to another argument. Just as her parents were so happy dancing together.

Learning this from her little sister, Shannon finds herself a mix of angry, powerless, and confused. Shannon asks, "Jealous of what?"

Grace shrugging, "That's what she believes."

"Grace, I have to get ready. Your drawings are amazing! Really good ideas. I hope Papa decides to follow them." Kissing Grace on her cheek and guiding her to her bedroom door.   Encouraging her baby sister, "Maybe one day you can design my house?"

"For sure! I love drawing -Oh! I should say designing houses." Grace moseys on to her bedroom with a validated sense of being seen.

Frank and Tommy have gone to the hardware and home improvement store. They go through the aisles buying nails, a second hammer, 2 x 4s of lumber that will serve to create walls for Tommy's closed-off studio space in the basement.

Father and son are spotted by *le Père Claude L'Heureux* from *l'Église Notre Dame.* A kind jovial man, like a young Santa Claus. He approaches them, *"Bonjour Monsieur Bailey, Bonjour Thomas! Cela fait longtemps que nous ne vous avons pas vu à Notre-Dame. Venez ce dimanche!"*

"Oui! Certainement!" Frank promises in his best French, smiling and waving. Then asking Tommy, "Did he tell us to come on Sunday?" Tommy answers, "Yes. And you agreed. So if I have to go to Church, I rather go there."

After a full day getting started on the new space, Frank and Tommy are up in the kitchen preparing sandwiches for their dinner.

Liliane visits them after having a peek, "I just went and saw what you boys have been doing. Impressive! Finally Tommy you'll be free to paint in your own space. Father Dale will be pleased. You can tell him tomorrow."

"We ran into *Curé Claude L'Heureux*. He invited us to *l'Église Notre Dame* tomorrow. It's good I practice my French for a project lead I want to take on at work. *Il faut faire des efforts.*"

"*Ah ouais?*" Liliane replies.

"We can all walk together?" Frank says suggesting she skip her lunch with you know who. Liliane says, "I'll see if Shannon wants to come with me."

Shannon has come back from her part time job. Liliane knocks on her door. "Hi Shannon, how was work today?"

"Good." Shannon replies wondering the source of her mother's interest.

Liliane sits on Shannon's bed. "We haven't spent much time together. Would you like to come with me to Church tomorrow?"

Shannon asks her, " Are you doing your lunch thing?"

Liliane, answers, "Yes. But you can go home with Nat."

"No. Nat's family is going to *l'Église Notre Dame.* Why don't you come with us to *Notre Dame?*"

Liliane, "I'm reading. So I have to be there and then there's lunch with Father Dale."

Shannon asks her mother directly, "What happens on Sundays and Thursdays with Father Dale? Why do you have to see him so much?"

There's a tension in the room. Liliane, feeling on the spot by Shannon and abandoned by Frank's decision to go to *l'Église Notre-Dame.* She is compelled to recruit Shannon's alliance.

"Shannon, I would like to talk to you about some grown-up things." Sighing, taking her time "You're older now. You should understand your father, he's been with other women. Maybe even after he married me."

Shannon suspicious of her mother's claim asks her, "He told you that?"

"Father Dale told me."

Shannon annoyed that her own mother would undermine her father in this way. Exasperated that her mother can't see how Father Dale is destroying her relationship with the only family she has.

"Why are you telling me this? Why did Father Dale tell you that?"

Liliane pleading with Shannon, "I just want you to know things are complicated and your father isn't perfect."

Shannon angered, "Yah! I know that. Neither are you, neither is anyone. What did Father Dale tell you and how can you believe it?"

Liliane answers, "I can believe it, because Frank confessed to him."

Shannon is appalled at the violation and betrayal. She iterates back to her mother, "Father Dale told you, your husband's private confession? And now you're telling me? What's wrong with you? Why? Why are you doing this?"

Liliane fixated on forging an alliance with Shannon tells her, "I would like you to come to Church with me."

"NO! No chance. Never will I go to mass with that idiot Father Dale! Who does he think he is?"
Liliane tells her, "Shannon! He's helped our family so much!"

Shannon is astonished at the insanity of this claim on the heel of such a betrayal of confidence. "How? How? How has he helped? You see him for Lunch on Sunday, then you have prayer meetings twice a week and Thursday afternoons? And the little love notes you hold onto in your room. Yes! I have seen them and read them!"

Liliane defensive dismissing the accusation, "We have a friendship. Father Dale is like our shepard. He loves us."

"Stop! He's a needy, lonely priest that tries to get all the wives infatuated with him! Emotionally, you are in an affair with him. At the very least emotionally and it's not right."

Liliane offended, "How dare you? I tried to have a grown-up conversation with you Shannon. I see you are not ready for that."

Shannon angry, " Apparently not, *MOTHER!*"

Liliane gets up and leaves the room, shutting the door behind her. Shannon goes to her desk and takes out a paper. Channeling her anger, she begins to draft a letter addressing it to the Bishop of the Catholic Diocese.

~ 17 ~

A RECKONING

The Chancellor is at his desk. He reaches for a bundle of envelopes held together with an elastic band. He unbinds them and shuffles through the collection, organizing according to the name of the recipient. He happens upon an inked envelope with an orderly script, possessing a youthful and feminine flair.

Taking a letter blade to the envelope, he reads the contents of a two paged hand written correspondence. The author a girl named, Shannon Bailey has listed serious grievances against a Father Dale. Requesting that he be defrocked for betraying her Father's private confession and for manipulating her mother's mindset.

The Chancellor fingers drums an irritated rhythm on the desk as he contemplates his duty. Picking up the phone he calls the Bishop to inform that he will be on his way to discuss a series of letters regarding a Father Lafferty. He pulls open his utility drawer at the centre of his desk to retrieve a key. Then takes that key to open another drawer at his desk, to pull out a box that only opens with a combination, to retrieve yet another key. That key opens a large walk in closet of shelving that stores files. He turns on the light and scans alphabetically over to a docket labelled 'Lafferty'.

He slips the latest correspondence into the docket. The Chancellor, in his black robe makes his way to the Bishop's office following a series of long elaborate hallways within the Seminary that serves as Roman Catholic Archdiocese of Québec.

Bowing at the doorway, the Chancellor informs, "We received a series of letters regarding Father Lafferty."

The Bishop asks, "What sort of indiscretions?"

The Chancellor opens the docket, pulling out each letter and providing a summary before handing the letter onto the Bishop says, "Letter one, is from a husband who came home unexpected during the day, to find his wife and Father Dale Lafferty in...well you can imagine."

The Bishop comments, "Sexual relations with a married women? Absolutely, not acceptable. Absolutely, no sex with women of child bearing age."

"There's a letter raising the concern inappropriate allocation of Church funds and donations. From a Mr. Bob Bergeron and a third letter from a young lady who claims that

Father Lafferty betrayed her father's confession by sharing the details with the wife, and her mother. She is demanding that Father Lafferty be transferred or defrocked for the manipulative mind control over her mother."

A fleeting grimace crosses the Bishop's face as he considers the allegations. "Not severe enough misconduct to be defrocked. If he confesses 'AGAIN' then we are required to mercifully forgive 'AGAIN'. Therefore, as we do, transfer him to another Diocese where he's out of range. There is a Parish in California, whose beloved brother recently returned to Our Lord."

The Bishop adds, "If we don't have to, don't let Father Lafferty know that we know. The last thing we want is to give him cause to leave the priesthood for one of these women."

About two weeks following the reception of Shannon's letter, Frank and the kids are in the front yard doing garden work after attending mass at *l'Église Notre Dame.*

Father Dale's car pulls up to the driveway with Liliane who is visibly distraught and crying. Curiously, Shannon looks to her brother and to her Father.

Father Dale walks slowly over to them on the lawn with Liliane who is holding his arm sobbing and wiping her nose with a squished up tissue.

"Good afternoon Frank, Tommy, Shannon, Grace. We've missed you these past weeks," Father Dale says meekly.

Frank excuses his absence in an eager French, *"Je pratique mon Français à Notre Dame."*

Liliane choked up blurts out, "He's leaving!"

Father Dale looking at each of them to announce earnestly, "It's true. I've been transferred to a Parish in California. I leave tomorrow."

Frank says as he removes his work gloves, "Oh! Is that so?" Restraining himself from saying *I guess I will have to find a new confessor.* Recognizing there's not a word he can sincerely or politely say. He decides to hold his hand out for a gentleman's good-bye.

With the exception of Liliane, the family is celebrating the good news. An optimism upon them that their family can be peaceful again without Father Dale's tampering of Liliane's mind.

Shannon feels a sense of justice served and encouragement that her letter made a difference. She did the right thing and time would prove it when her parents could recover from this outsider's interference.

Over the next few weeks the family comes together. They walk to the French Sunday Mass at *l'Église Notre Dame*. Grace catches up to her violin practices and even plays a tune along with Shannon at the piano. To keep him out of trouble, Tommy has been paired with an Art Mentor who teaches at the University that Frank found for him. And while it has taken Liliane time to adjust, she begins to explore her creativity in the projects she always enjoyed before *you know who.*

With enough time and peace, Frank and Liliane reconcile to each other on a weekend hiking trip in the Laurentian Mountains. An overdue cabin escape rekindling their mutual desire for closeness.

~ 18 ~

THE HOOVER TECHNIQUE

Liliane has come to smile at her husband and find gratitude for their rekindled romance. Seeing her husband and herself in a different light. Bringing about a needed shift in perspective and identity. Inspired to organize the clutter of drawers in her bedroom, she comes across the book, *The Thorn Birds*, and the little notes and small cards from Father Dale. These trigger an unpleasant guilt for the betrayal of her love and devotion to her husband and family.

She gathers every evidence of a time when her mind was hijacked. Bringing these to the backyard BBQ, she douses the book and the papers with alcohol and lights a match. Watching the flames eat up the paper with a moving ember turning into black ash. Letting go she asks herself *What on earth happened to me?*

Just as Liliane believed the past was now behind her, the Postman arrives to hand her the mail. There it is a post card from Lake Tahoe, California. The message on the reverse is brief,

"Liliane,
Something I need to tell you,
Love Dale"

His message is followed by a phone number for Liliane to call.

When Frank comes home from work, Liliane is ecstatic and all over the place. An unpleasant nervous energy Frank hasn't witnessed in her for some time. She tells him, "I have news!" Her eyes are wide and glossed over and he is dreading what she 's about to say next.

"Father Dale's invited me to California! I've never been to California!" She is manic in her excitement.

"He told my story to the Bishop. *To the Bishop*! I have been invited to host a Women's retreat! A retreat! Can you believe it Frank? Me, host a retreat? In California?"

The nightmare revisiting, this time with the echo of Dr. Rosenthal's voice in Frank's head;

"How do you think he maintains this level of influence?"

ABOUT THE AUTHOR

E.G. Boylan is the pen name for artist and illustrator, Elisabeth Boylan. Born and raised in Montréal, Québec, Elisabeth pursued post-secondary studies in Lille, France followed by Fine Art Studies at Emily Carr University of Art and Design in Vancouver, BC.

An outdoor enthusiast and snowboarder, she made a home for herself on the West Coast for twenty-three years, living in Vancouver, Nelson and Whistler, British Columbia. Finally returning to her home province to continue her creative practice from her studio in Québec City.

Thorns Of Piety is a début novella, a 'tramedy' work of fiction inspired by the author's experiences and observations from her childhood in Québec.

Randall James grew up on spectacular Cape Breton Island, NS, and now resides on beautiful Vancouver Island, BC. He likes to walk along the shore in the day and gaze at stars at night.